FINAL WARNING

A flock of hungry sky eagles was pursuing the *Blackbird* with a vengeance.

Cox's thoughts turned to the single piece of ordnance he carried onboard—a long-range Highwire ALCM. But the brilliant, terminally guided missile would only be able to take out one of the fighters.

Just then, he made visual contact with the two jets vectoring toward him. They were *Flankers*, powerful and fast, bristling with the most sophisticated rockets in the AA class. They were waggling their wings in the international code, signaling him to land the black stealth ship.

Cox knew this would be the last warning he was likely to receive ...

BANDIT

DAVID
ALEXANDER

AVON BOOKS ◆ NEW YORK

BANDIT is an original publication of Avon Books. This work has never before appeared in book form. This work is a novel. Any similarity to actual persons or events is purely coincidental. Though some names in the book are real, the events surrounding them are purely fictional.

AVON BOOKS
A division of
The Hearst Corporation
1350 Avenue of the Avenues
New York, New York 10019

Copyright © 1994 by David Alexander
Published by arrangement with the author
Library of Congress Catalog Card Number: 94-94075
ISBN: 0-380-76860-7

First Avon Books Printing: September 1994

AVON TRADEMARK REG. U.S. PAT. OFF. AND IN OTHER COUNTRIES, MARCA REGISTRADA, HECHO EN U.S.A.

Printed in the U.S.A.

RA 10 9 8 7 6 5 4 3 2 1

"It's a bloody miracle that one of these eggs has not gotten loose in the last forty years. The subject of control over nuclear weapons is so awful a problem that there aren't any real solutions to them, and you can't relax about it at all."

—*Former CIA Director William E. Colby commenting on a report that Soviet President Mikhail Gorbachev had lost control of nuclear forces during the August 1991 Kremlin coup.*

Author's Note

The aircraft described in this book is technically an SR-71A. However, for purposes of clarity, the designations "SR," "SR-71" and "SR-71A" are used interchangeably throughout.

D.A.

Preface

In October of 1989, the U.S. Air Force officially suspended flight operations of its Lockheed SR-71 (Strategic Reconnaissance) Blackbird aircraft.

At that time, the USAF began the progressive phasing-out of the approximately twenty-five[1] SR-71s which had been operational up to that time.

Apart from two SR-71s detached to forward observation bases at Kadena, Japan, and Mildenhall, England, the rest of the fleet of Blackbirds was mothballed, and TR-1 and U2 reconnaissance aircraft deployed in those few instances where satellite reconnaissance was deemed unsuitable to the mission role.

The proliferation of satellite-based, high-definition surveillance platforms in polar and geosynchronous orbits, combined with the extremely high costs of operating and maintaining the Blackbird fleet, was cited by the Air Force as making the SR-71 redundant for the purposes of strategic reconnaissance.

However that may be, the SR-71 Blackbird is unquestionably one of the most mission-capable aircraft ever flown, and in an era of increasing geopolitical instability, the reports of its demise may be somewhat premature.

---

[1]This is an educated guess. The actual number of planes in service has never been made public.

PROLOGUE

December 1989

December 1989

Cinched up within the black metal dagger hurtling through darkness at the speed of a bullet leaving the muzzle of a gun, his body encased in an air-conditioned flight suit, Colonel Dan Cox kept his hand on the joystick and his eyes on the SR-71 spy aircraft's AN/ASG-18 long-range, look-up/look-down coherent pulse doppler radar scope.

In the RSO's cockpit aft of the pilot's, Cox's backseater, a CIA flight technician named Holloway, monitored the performance of the most accurate photosurveillance cameras ever built, cameras capable of recording objects on the ground with detailed resolution at the supersonic speeds the SR traveled.

Cruising at a ninety-thousand-foot flight ceiling, at the upward limits of the aircraft's performance envelope, the SR owned the skies, and the earth below could hold no secrets from her far-seeing gaze.

The ultramarine edge of space loomed on his forward horizon as Cox pitched the SR-71 into a new course heading which would vector the spyplane into a high-altitude overfly of Panama City, Panama. According to the aircraft's inertial navigation system, ETA was in five minutes.

The SR-71 Blackbird handled stable as a table as

Cox began a decel/descent from full afterburner flight to a speed in the low Mach numbers and an eighty-thousand-foot flight ceiling. Doing so would enable the sleek black spyplane's multimillion-dollar photoreconnaissance cameras to take successive frames of their targets below at optimum resolution for each exposure.

The SR's sophisticated ELINT gear, located in hull blisters and antenna dents positioned along the plane's chined fuselage, would also commence a broad spectrum scan of the electronic environment. Intelligence collected on the mission would be forwarded to the National Reconnaissance Office at Meade for analysis.

These data would be of critical importance in the final planning stages of the invasion of Panama. One of the primary goals of the classified recon mission—code-named Operation Just Cause—was something which had not been attempted for at least forty-five years, since Otto Skorzeny and a band of Nazi commandos had used glider aircraft to break Italian Duce Benito Mussolini out of Gran Sasso Prison, where he had been held in the wake of Italy's surrender.

If newly elected President George Bush had his way, Manuel Antonio Noriega, the military dictator of Panama, would soon be abducted from his own country and incarcerated in an American prison.

The SR-71's photoreconnaissance mission above the skies of Panama had been ordered to gather high-resolution image intelligence of Noriega's headquarters, the fortified complex in the heart of Panama City known as the *comandancia.*

Special forces teams, comprised of elements of Army Rangers, Navy SEALS and Delta Force personnel, were already standing ready for deployment to the strike zone. The work product of the SR-71's mission would provide these SOF elements with the high-grade intelligence which would enable them to storm the *coman-*

dancia and engineer the Noriega snatch, should this contingency be deemed operationally sound by the planners of Just Cause.

Although Cox flew the SR for the CIA but was not himself an Agency asset, his reconnaissance systems operator, or RSO, did work for the Agency. The task of the RSO, seated behind the pilot's cockpit, was to manage the computers which controlled the four sequenced, high-resolution LOROP cameras positioned at port and starboard of the SR's underbelly, the Itek optical bar camera just aft of its nose and the spyplane's blistered ELINT sensors located at various points on its fuselage.

Cox's backseater was as capable as he was close-mouthed. Cox had flown with Holloway before on missions over and around the skies of Vietnam, Afghanistan, Russia and Grenada. For all the mission time they had logged together, the RSO and Cox had hardly interacted, although Cox sometimes wondered if his own personality had as much to do with this condition as the spooks' tradecraft, which demanded an often paranoiac-seeming code of silence.

At forty-seven years of age, Daniel Cox had earned himself a reputation for two things: piloting and being a pugnacious S.O.B.

A muscular man of middle height, with blunt-angled features and sharp green eyes, Cox still retained the physique of a cruiserweight boxer and the natural aggressiveness that went along with it. He was supremely capable at what he did, and the mere fact of his survival in flying the most dangerous missions in the history of military aviation was testament to this fact.

Which meant that Cox was also an anachronism. For in an age of push-button warfare, the warrior had been reduced in status to a surrogate for instruments of mechanized killing.

Keyhole, Rhyolite, Magnum and Lacrosse-class intelligence satellites had slowly taken over the mission for which the SR-71 fleet had originally been designed and built over two decades before.

The spysats had proved themselves capable of doing the job more cheaply and faster, delivering real-time intelligence telemetry, whereas the lead time for data brought back by an SR run dictated that product would not be available for analysis until several hours after collection.

Only the previous week Cox had learned that the SR-71 was to be phased out of active service within a year and its role relegated to the new, unmanned orbiting eyes in the sky.

He had decided that both the sleek black covert reconnaissance aircraft and he himself would share the same fate.

Cox had been offered a desk job at Company headquarters in Langley, Virginia, but had turned it down, opting for early retirement instead. The age of Stealth and LaCrosse would continue without him.

Holloway's voice in Cox's helmet earphones brought him abruptly back to the present. The Company photoreconnaissance systems operator was requesting a course correction in order to make another pass over the target zone from a different overfly angle.

"I'd like to execute an approach from a sixty-degree heading this time," Holloway said. "I want to get some additional coverage of certain features of the southeastern grid quadrant."

"Roger on that," Cox told the RSO via helmet commo and executed a tight, low-g turn which brought the SR-71 back around for another pass over the *comandancia* area.

"Okay. Guess that wraps it up," the RSO said when this final surveillance pass had been completed. "Let's head for home base."

Cox set a course heading for the covert airstrip in the Florida panhandle at which the Company and NSA had established a joint forward observation base. He throttled the SR back up, fire-walling the afterburner, satisfying himself that his fuel reserves for the return leg of the transoceanic flight were adequate, and began the hour-long run back to base at a high-altitude ceiling.

Before dawn of the following morning, Operation Just Cause would commence and U.S. Apache helicopters would own the skies over Panama City.

Not too long after America's assault on the Central American republic, owing in large part to the intelligence gathered by the SR-71's high-altitude photoreconnaissance flight, General Manuel Antonio Noriega, President of Panama, would find himself in the custody of United States federal marshals and his dictatorial regime permanently dismantled.

PART ONE
1992

Trip Wire

I

Eastern Russian Republic, C.I.S.

Its armored hull painted in a Warsaw Pact woodland camouflage pattern, the BMP negotiated the steep, timber-flanked mountain road.

Ahead of the tracked vehicle rolled a military staff car equipped with a pintle-mounted 7.62 mm RPK machine gun, and behind it there trundled a two-and-a-half-ton army transport truck carrying a platoon of infantry soldiers attired in the camouflage battle dress of mountain assault troops. A ZSU-23-4 triple-A gun platform followed at the rear of the column, its multiple barrels covered with protective canvas tarp.

Zulu time was 0400 hours. Overhead, the moonless night sky was as clear as an inverted glass bowl placed against a background of black felt. The special mechanized unit had remained hidden during the daylight hours and throughout most of the night, mobilizing according to a precisely coordinated schedule.

On reaching its destination, the column halted and the troops jumped from their seats in the transport to set up a security perimeter. Porting AKM assault rifles, they stood guard over the BMP while the ZSU-23-4 triple-A unit's multiple barrels were aimed skyward.

In the command, control and communications center located within the armored hull of the tracked vehicle, technical officers Dmitri Zhegalov and Leonid Trusov were seated at consoles running along either bulkhead in which multiple arrays of computer screens had suddenly come alive, displaying an assortment of tactical data.

TRACKING.
ETA TO OVERPASS: 5340 SECONDS.

Suddenly flashing on the screen, the confirmation-alert message produced an instant surge of adrenaline in both officers. It told Zhegalov that the platform's long-range multibeam search radars had locked onto the target signature which belonged to the objective of the covert predawn mission.

One hundred fifty miles above the surface of the earth, the satellite's low-apogee polar orbit would arc it overhead in the space of roughly ten more minutes.

A critical point in the mission would soon be reached.

Zhegalov next scanned the rack-mounted VDT on the console before him, which provided him with data concerning the energization process. Readings from the terminal indicated that the BMP's bank of lithium power cells was charged at near-capacity voltage levels.

This unit would be fully operational in just under eight minutes. This would provide sufficient lead time for any final azimuth corrections to the combat platform elevating mast to be input at the console.

Zhegalov did not believe that such corrections would be necessary, however. On all previous missions the fail-soft, fault-tolerant software and hardware had performed without a hitch. The chief systems officer had no doubt that the same would apply now.

At 0409 hours, the final main-systems energizing and

target-acquisition sequencing procedures had been initialized. Zhegalov and his deputy systems officer, Trusov, kept their eyes riveted to the banks of multiple display rasters bolted into the console's rack mounts, their faces limned with constantly shifting bands of color reflected from the screens before them.

As they went about their tasks, the thirty-foot elevating mast, which had reached full extension atop the tracked armored vehicle, was jockeyed into place by hydraulic elevating actuators and pull rods, kept in alignment by constant corrections by highly accurate millimeter wave tracking radars.

AUTOMATIC TARGET SEQUENCER LOCKED ON. INITIALIZING MAIN POWER SUPPLY.

Zhegalov saw the glowing blue icon designating the target signature materialize at twelve o'clock on the computer-enhanced color radar display raster. The countdown sequence flashed on a liquid crystal digital readout mounted at the side of the scope panel.

When the automatic launch sequencer had ticked down to the zero mark, Zhegalov and his deputy systems officer heard the high-pitched whine of the BMP's heavy-duty step-up transformers discharging almost a million kilovolts of electrical power that energized the combat platform atop the elevating mast.

The infantry troops that stood guard over the BMP also heard this sound, and they saw the brilliant red lance line of coherent radiation suddenly materialize from the combat platform and shoot upward into the blackness of the moonless night sky. The ruler-straight beam continued to lance skyward for several seconds, then abruptly disappeared as the dynamo whine skirled down to inaudibility.

Inside the BMP's command, control and communications center, Zhegalov observed the glowing blue icon representing the target suddenly turn yellow.

ENGAGEMENT SUCCESSFUL.
TARGET DESTROYED.

Zhegalov input a coded sequence at the keypad in front of him which would immediately shut down all combat systems.

Elapsed mission time had been a little over twenty minutes according to the Zulu mission clock. Despite the hardened electronic systems of the BMP, Zhegalov knew that there would almost certainly be some TEMPEST leakage into the environment, enough of it to render the platform observable to ECM seekers deployed by hostile forces and targeted for a strike.

With the elevating mast atop the BMP now retracted and again nestled in its protective seam, Zhegalov ordered the infantry troops back into the transport and the column to immediately extract from the op zone.

If it failed to do so, then the non-radiation-silent unit would present a soft, stationary target for those who had every reason to want it destroyed, quickly and—above all—silently.

2

Fort Meade, Maryland

The headquarters of the National Security Agency, or
NSA, which oversees electronic intelligence gathering
and has oversight over CIA, DIA and other federal
agencies in this critical area, is a collection of unim-
posing buildings located in the exurban sprawl that
has grown up between Washington, D.C., and Balti-
more, Maryland.

The only clue to the nature of the clandestine activities which take place within the installation is the clus-
ters of antennae and radar masts that bristle from the
bland architecture.

The array of electronic and computer systems housed
inside those buildings, though, is anything but unimpos-
ing. In fact, the NSA's Meade complex is said to con-
tain the most elaborate assortment of ELINT hardware
to be found anywhere in the world, including a Cray
supercomputer powerful enough to monitor worldwide
phone traffic and record conversations filtered by specific words or phrases such as "CIA," "wet job" or
"covert strike."

At one of the consoles in the darkened command
center, orbital surveillance officer Ron Gentry was
maintaining a remote vigil on the telemetry intelligence,
or TELINT, originating from one of three KH-12 Key-

hole intelligence satellites deployed in geostationary orbits, his fingers hovering over the assortment of dedicated keyboards in front of him as his trained eyes
scanned the multiple graphic display screens feeding
him both regular position updates and telemetry from
the Keyhole to which he was assigned.

The KH-12's official NSA designation was 1989-418P,
the serial number indicating that it was launched on
April 18, 1989, from Patrick Air Force Base at Cape Ca-
naveral, Florida. The 3.5-ton intelsat was currently at the
perigee of orbit number 6951, its orbital trajectory sling-
shoting it across the northern edge of the Eurasian landmass at supersonic speeds.

Keyhole's mission was to monitor the SS-18, SS-20
and rail-mobile SS-24 missile installations known to be
situated at Murukta, Peleduj, Skovoradino and several
other locations in the northeastern sector of the Russian
heartland; these sites lay within the seventy-mile swath
which the Keyhole's photoreconnaissance and infrared
sensors were capable of scanning in a single pass.

Along with North Dakota in the United States, this
area of the former Soviet Union shared the distinction
of having the greatest number of nuclear warheads per
square mile of any region on the planet stored thereon.

Like the array of spy satellites being monitored by
other systems officers at other consoles scattered
throughout the darkened room, the Keyhole had been
placed in orbit by NASA and would function as a critical component of the newly ratified U.S.-Soviet Start
Treaty verification oversight requirement.

Spying had long since ceased to be solely an art
practiced in the back alleys of the world. It was now a
science, and one that was vital to maintaining a new
and fragile bilateral peace.

HIGH LEVEL FAILURE: CODE 287.

Gentry's face twisted up in a sudden grimace. As the error message flashed on the screen, the Keyhole's position icon had suddenly undergone a phase shift. Originally blue, designating normal operating parameters, the icon now glowed white and flashed on and off.

This phase shift indicated a system error, and the error code 287 further indicated the existence of a critical problem with operating ROM of the KH-12's central processing unit.

Gentry input a series of keystrokes and attempted to restart Keyhole via the intelsat's redundant on-board backup systems.

After a few minutes, trying various remote fixes to jump-start the fail-soft, fault-tolerant systems engineered into the hardware which controlled the satellite, the tech continued to receive abort messages.

Reluctantly, Gentry came to the conclusion that the satellite was down and there was nothing that he could do about it.

Some minutes later, Tom Chang, the crew chief assigned to the orbital surveillance intelligence section, punched up the hard data from Gentry's equipment in the form of a computer printout. The printout showed Chang that the Keyhole had suddenly and inexplicably ceased to function. Chang, a dour-faced Agency lifer with a disposition to go with his appearance, cursed a blue streak.

These data being shown him represented a statistical impossibility which his analytical mind refused to accept.

The sophisticated PHOTINT satellite was equipped with redundant backup systems and designed to automatically shunt over to these if any single one should fail.

One or several of these fault-tolerant features would normally remain functional despite any contingency short of a devastating event. Systems redundancy ensured that survivability was built into the satellites' operating architecture.

What was even more disturbing to Chang was that this satellite was the third orbital surveillance platform that, over the course of the past twenty-one days, had suddenly ceased functioning under unexplainable circumstances.

This was a fact known only to Chang and those higher up on the NSA's chain of command, but was kept secret from the ground support staff which monitored the spysats.

Such a high systems-failure rate could not even be remotely attributed to normal operational circumstances. The odds against three orbital intelligence platforms suddenly ceasing to function were too astronomical to warrant consideration. But the inescapable conclusion was equally unthinkable: *sombody was deliberately tampering with those satellites.*

Prague, Czechoslovakia

Pavel Novotny knew that the men who had hunted him from Kiev to St. Petersburg and now to Prague would soon overtake him.

Though the former Sov Bloc secret police networks had been among the first institutions of the old regimes to be dismantled in the wake of the revolutionary events which had first swept the Soviet Union's outer satellites and then the U.S.S.R. itself, the underlying infrastructure would take decades to wither away. The

reach of the "Vlasti"—the former holders of power—
was still exceedingly long.

The old guard of Communist apparatchiks even now
remained a cogent force in the affairs of Eastern Eu-
rope. They were as much a force in the new order as
the outwardly repentant but secretly recalcitrant Nazis
had been in Germany after the end of the Second World
War.

No one could be trusted. The old hierarchy was still
intact, though gone to ground in clandestine Party cells.
As the intelligence Pavel possessed would make clear,
these forces were moving toward a coup d'état with
worldwide consequences, one which, unlike the Kremlin coup of a previous August, would not end in dismal
failure.

Pavel was the bearer of a secret which made him
highly expendable. The opposition would go to extreme
lengths to silence the messenger.

Pavel knew he had to act quickly. The message he
carried required transmission to his CIA handler before
the *boyevaya* came for him, and the device he had retrieved from the dead drop in Krizovnicka Street would
allow him to do so. Only minutes remained, perhaps
less, before he was liquidated.

The pouch flap opened with the rasp of Velcro fas-
teners separating and Pavel removed the compact PRC
319 burst transmitter unit from its protective foam co-
coon. He flipped on the power button and moments
later saw the READY message on the PRC 319's four-
line, light-emitting diode screen.

Pavel typed out the three-thousand-character situation
report on the unit's keyboard and saved it to inboard
CMOS memory. He played the sitrep back, satisfied
himself that it was accurate, then depressed the confirm
key, followed by the send key.

The TRANSMISSION SUCCESSFUL message on the unit's

screen confirmed that the sitrep had been compressed down into a high-frequency coded radio signal of a few seconds' duration.

There was virtually no way for the signal to be intercepted, much less deciphered. Electronic handshaking protocols assured Pavel that the orbiting comsat to which it was being beamed had picked up the transmission and was already relaying it to the NSA listening post for the Balkan region, in Ankhara, Turkey.

Pavel stuffed clothing into an overnight bag and prepared to flee the safe house in Prague's Old Town section where he had taken refuge for the past twenty-four hours. A warning call from one of Pavel's cutouts had come only minutes ago, and Pavel knew that the flat was no longer safe. The killers who pursued him were closing in and he had to run.

A sudden knock at the door made him start, and his throat went suddenly dry as an old sock.

Too soon, Pavel thought to himself, *too damned soon.*

Only a few more minutes and he might have survived. The knock came again as Pavel set the digital timer on the button charge which would destroy the PRC 319 and render retrieval of the message he had sent from its microprocessor impossible.

With one foot on the fire escape, Pavel was edging through the window he had raised as the flat's door burst open and two *boyevaya* in black leather jackets swung the muzzles of silenced semiautomatic pistols this way and that, seeking target acquisition, quickly sighting on the escaping figure framed against the skyline of Prague.

Now completely out the window and standing on the slatted metal platform beyond, Pavel heard the whine of a ricocheting 9 mm round, followed a pulsebeat later by the dull crump of the Semtex plastic explosive detonating as the booby-trapped burst transmitter unit's timer ran down to zero.

As Pavel hustled down the metal stairs and jumped to the flagstones of the alley below, he heard shouts from the apartment above as the *boyevaya* hesitated between trying to retrieve the demolished burst transmitter and pursuing the fleeing CIA ground asset.

Pavel ran for his life toward the mouth of the alley, but stopped short as the silhouette loomed into view.

The blond man in the windbreaker raised the weapon clutched in a two-handed grip. It was a small Crvena Zastava semiautomatic, and the stubby black silencer jutting from its muzzle did little to alter the gun's compact profile.

The pistol coughed once and Pavel fell to the cobblestone streets with fragments of a dumdum round buried in his brain, a casualty of a war which had officially ceased to be fought, a victim of forces which were said to no longer exist in a world finally, though not fully or truly, at peace.

3

Eastern Russian Republic, C.I.S.

General Fyodor Ivanovich Aleksiev walked the compound on one of his nightly inspection tours. The base was quiet now, and the frigid wind swept down from the high peaks of the towering mountains beyond the perimeter fence with the sharpness of an eagle's talons.

Local legends claimed that if one listened carefully enough, one could indeed hear the voices of the dead whom the mountains had claimed.

Aleksiev believed that there was truth in this legend. In the keening of the night wind the general could plainly hear the voices of dead men.

But he knew that these voices came from another source, one deep within him. They sprang from the depths of his own mind and they belonged to the soldiers whom he had abandoned to their fates in the desolate mountains of Afghanistan many years before.

In the years since the Soviet pullout from the Muslim nation flanking the U.S.S.R.'s southern border, the general had lost the need for sleep almost entirely.

Specters haunted his dreams and would not give him peace. They were the demons rising out of the past, ghosts of dead Spetsnaz who returned to his sleep to point their skeletal fingers accusingly at him.

"Why did you leave us here?" the dead men implored Aleksiev. "Why did you leave us to die in this accursed place?"

It was not Aleksiev's fault that they had died, the general answered the dead Voiska Spetsialnogo Nazacheniya, special-purpose forces troops. It was the nature of war, he told them.

But the ghoulish skeletons would not listen to him, even as the general pleaded with them to understand. It had been the weaklings in the Kremlin who had lost faith in their ability to succeed, he continued to protest to the rotting legions of the departed, their fleshless skulls and sinewless limbs still attired in the camouflage fatigues of Spetsnaz personnel.

It was the weak fools who had not had the will to fight, who had allowed them to become mired in a war of attrition which they could not hope to win, he screamed at the damned souls that had returned to torment him.

But the ghostly accusers would have none of the general's protests, and they closed in around him, reaching out with skeletal hands to pull him toward their hideous ranks, dragging him to an open mass grave as Aleksiev smelled the noxious odors of their rotting corpse flesh and awoke with his own screams echoing in the stillness of the night.

On awakening, Aleksiev would dress hastily and leave his billet, knowing that sleep would not again return. He would go out into the night and brood amidst the towering mountains where the souls of the dead looked down on him with unquenchable hatred.

Afghanistan had been a turning point for the Soviet Union, a crossroads at which the empire had taken the first steps along the road that by now had brought it to within an ace of complete ruination.

Aleksiev would not allow either the fools in the Center or the traitors in the republics to complete the dismantling of his beloved Rodina—his Motherland. The course they had chosen in their blindness played directly into the hands of the Americans.

What did the Americans offer in exchange for the Motherland's dissolution? *Nothing* was the answer.

Nothing except for the imperialistic domination to which they had already subjected the rest of the world. Across the country, the morally bankrupt puppets were toadying to the Americans and would receive only promises in return for their groveling. The Americans were treacherous and greedy. They could never be trusted to do anything but plunder his homeland.

There was still time to save the Motherland. Precious little time, Aleksiev knew, and it was dwindling with each passing tick of the clock. But he would use whatever time there was left. He would alter the course of history by the application of his iron will.

It was not inevitable by any means that Russia go the way of the rest of the world. She could still survive with her own identity intact.

If he acted quickly.

If he acted boldly.

Aleksiev turned and looked up at the mountains that surrounded him on all sides and listened again to the voices of Spetsnaz ghosts carried on the keening wind. He would avenge their deaths, he promised them. They would not have died in vain.

Maybe then his nightmares would cease.

The White House

In the underground crisis room of the National Security Council, President Webster Bancroft sat facing the Secretary of State, the Director of Central Intelligence, the Director of the National Security Agency and various other personnel, including his National Security Advisor and his Communications Director.

The brief which the intelligence people were handing the President was nothing short of incredible. In the space of a few short weeks, three of the country's most sophisticated ELINT, PHOTINT and SIGINT satellites—Ferret, Keyhole and the advanced Vortex-class orbital platforms—had been taken out of commission.

Chagrined, the President listened to his advisors present their reports on the developing crisis.

"Excuse me, gentlemen," Bancroft said to the assemblage and then left the room. Seating himself by a secure phone with automatic call-taping capability in the antechamber to the briefing room, the President placed an urgent call to Sergei Pavlovich, the President of the Russian commonwealth.

The President's "telephone diplomacy" style had been highly successful in welding together the grand alliance which had helped win the campaign in the Gulf, and his "palocracy" style of interaction with heads of state had already become something of a media cliché.

The Russian leader came to the phone minutes later. Bancroft's opposite number sounded as though he had been asleep. Because of the eight-hour differential between Washington and Moscow time, Sergei Pavlovich had been awakened from the troubled dreams of a man with weighty matters on his mind.

"I'm sorry to disturb you, Sergei, but we have a problem," the President said bluntly. "American intelligence satellites are being blinded—and in at least one case destroyed—as they pass over your country. We are gravely concerned by these events. Can you tell me anything that might clarify our understanding of the situation?"

"You must believe me when I say that I have no knowledge of these serious matters," responded the

Russian leader, used by now to the U.S. President's blunt, personal interactive style. "We here in the Commonwealth are as much in the dark as you are."

"Can this really be true, Sergei?" Bancroft pressed the Russian leader. "Am I to believe that an undertaking of such magnitude could be taking place without your direct knowledge?"

"You do not know, then?" Pavlovich answered with a mirthless laugh after a beat. "No, of course you don't. We have been keeping it a secret. You see, Webster, our satellites, they too have been blinded. Were it not for the fact that your fighter-launched ASAT weapons operate by destroying rather than by merely blinding, we would have suspected an American hand in the matter. As it is, we are as mystified as you are."

"I see. Then we are both dealing with an unknown and serious factor," Bancroft replied, signing off by saying, "I'll get back to you, Sergei, if there are any new developments. Please keep me informed, and again, my apologies for this disturbance."

Bancroft returned directly to the NSC meeting room and minutes later faced the assemblage therein. He related the gist of his conversation with the former Soviet President to his eagerly attentive listeners.

"Well, I frankly don't believe it," Conrad Lowell, the Secretary of Defense, told the President. "Pavlovich *must* know. The assets necessary to bring off the neutralization of our orbital surveillance capability alone would require sanctions at the highest operational levels."

"I pray you're wrong," said the President. "However, we must now turn our attention to the question of how to respond to this threat. How badly is our surveillance capability hurt?" This question was directed to NSA Director Justin Slattery.

"Mr. President," Slattery replied. "Quantitatively

speaking, our satellite capability has barely been touched. However, *qualitatively* it has been severely compromised. The three orbital intelligence platforms we're missing are the most advanced in our inventory. Indeed, without them the data we have to work with is of an unacceptably inferior grade. Their loss presents us with a significant setback."

"I see," Bancroft said, his face grave. "And yet it is critical that we obtain breaking intelligence on whether or not these disablings were effected in preparation for some belligerent move. Have HUMINT assets been tasked?"

"Sir, in the wake of recent events in Russia and a lessening of U.S.-Russian tensions, our HUMINT capability is at an all-time low. However, what my people find ominous is the killing of a Czech operative in Prague who, reports indicate, had transmitted preliminary intelligence of high grade and was about to follow on with significant breaking intelligence."

"We're back to square one, then," Bancroft stated. "It is imperative that we obtain high-grade intelligence on this crisis before acting. Bill," the President next said to the DCI, "it looks like the ball's in your court."

The Director of Central Intelligence took the floor. William "Wild Bill" Farragutt was the third Wild Bill after Donovan and Casey to head the CIA. He was known for favoring exotic covert operations as the solution to most crises, and, as Casey before him, was said to possess what the Germans called *fingerspitzengefuehl*—an intuitive feel for the clandestine.

"Sir, we have received intelligence from several agents in place," he began. "The finished intelligence tends to confirm that the Russian President might not be holding the reigns of power. Another coup may be imminent. I have, however, outlined some recommendations which I would relate to you if you will permit me."

"Let's hear it, Bill," Bancroft acknowledged.

"Mr. President, what we propose is to use our only existent surveillance capability, a manned reconnaissance aircraft, to overfly Russian airspace at high altitude and bring back intelligence data."

"You mean our F117A Stealth fighters?" the President asked perplexedly, not getting the DCI's point.

"No, sir, I don't," the DCI answered immediately. "The Stealth's forward-looking radars are not up to the task. As you know, their performance was disappointing during Desert Storm and it was necessary to insert special forces ground units in order to locate and illuminate targets. This and a number of other factors, including the fact that its mission role does not support the high-resolution photosurveillance required, disqualify the F117A."

"What, then?" the President asked Farragutt.

"The SR-71 Blackbird, sir," the DCI replied. "The spyplane which was officially mothballed three years ago. It is still as fast as or faster than anything the Russians—or ourselves, for that matter—have in the sky. It can also fly higher than most conventional aircraft and it has proved itself over time as being able to handle missions of extremely long duration."

The President considered the DCI's proposal for a few minutes. As a former CIA director, he knew the value of the SR's intelligence firsthand and had never been in favor of cutting the Blackbird program entirely.

Despite the high ground maintenance and operating costs necessary to keep the fleet of recon aircraft flying, Bancroft had believed that there was still a place for the SR in America's intelligence assets inventory and had bowed to Congressional budget axe-swingers only in an effort to salvage other programs he considered still more important.

An old Navy pilot himself, he admired the beautiful, functional aircraft whose intelligence-gathering capability had made it one of the trump cards America had played in order to score its overwhelming victory in the Cold War.

"What about Aurora and JSTARS?" Bancroft countered. "Can't those systems do the job?"

"Negative, sir," was Farragutt's response. "From both logistical and technological standpoints, I'm afraid neither is an option."

"Can we field the plane in time?" he asked Farragutt.

"Yes, I believe we can, sir." The DCI went on. "We have prepared a feasibility study, which you have in front of you. To synopsize, what it proposes is to retrofit an existing SR-71 with state-of-the-art equipment, modify its air chine somewhat for additional stealth capability and then send it out to do what it does best."

The President thumbed through the hundred-odd-page Umbra-coded report in front of him on the polished teak desk.

"I'll get back to you later today, after I've had a chance to go over this," he shortly told the DCI. "But one thing, Bill—who are we gonna get to fly the darned thing? Do we even have any pilots available anymore who are experienced enough to handle the mission?"

"I have a pilot in mind," the DCI told the President right away, secretly dreading that the CinC had asked that question.

The man he had in mind was the best there was. But Dan Cox was also a died-in-the-wool sonofabitch.

"It's doable, sir," he concluded and left the NSC briefing room. Now all he had to do was convince retired Colonel Dan Cox of the same thing.

4

Bali, Indonesia

Suteng handed the earthenware jug of consecrated water to the American garbed in the colorful native dress of the Balinese. Holy to the Ashanta branch of Hinduism, water is used on virtually every occasion, and for that reason Ashanta has come to be known as "the water religion."

In the present case, the purpose of the holy water was to cleanse the recently exhumed skeletal remains of Suteng's maternal aunt, who had been interred for over seven years.

Cox accepted the water offering with a small bow of gratitude, which was the traditional response. It was a great honor for a foreigner to be allowed to directly participate in this holiest of Balinese rituals, and Cox was aware of the privilege he was being accorded.

In Bali the cremation of the dead is a communal activity. Sometimes a decade will pass before the burning ceremony is able to take place.

During this time, artisans have been busy fashioning elaborate, colorful crypts in the forms of fantastic animals and bizarre gods, made out of papier-mâché and balsa wood in which to house the exhumed bones of the sacred dead.

When the remains are disinterred, they are placed in

the flamboyant crypts, then brought with ritualistic displays of song and dance to the site where the mass cremations will be carried out.

This is a time of feasting and celebration. The dead will finally be given the honors they have awaited for so long, while the living, having performed their sacred obligation, are then free to engage in protracted festivities.

Cox sprinkled the consecrated water from the earthen jug on the skeleton before the bones of Suteng's relative were placed in their crypt—this one in the form of a winged dragon—with great reverence by the extended family.

By now the procession toward the consecrated grove where the burnings were to take place had already begun. Cox accompanied the procession, joining in the mass chant of ancient Balinese hymns as best he could.

As he participated in the festival of cremation, watching the smoke of the burning papier-mâché crypts ascend to the clear blue sky amid the overhanging fronds of thirty-foot-high coconut palms, two casually dressed men in sunglasses broke from the crowd of camcorder-pointing tourists observing from the sidelines.

"Colonel Daniel Cox?" one of them asked as they approached him.

Turning at the sound of his name, Cox looked the men over. Despite their leisure clothes, they had the unmistakable appearance of spooks.

The Company went to great lengths to condition its assets to display blank expressions and keep their emotions from registering on their faces.

Unfortunately, this training also announced the presence of field assets as clearly as might a neon sign.

"Hey, I like those shades, chief," Cox replied to the first spook, reaching out with surprising speed and taking the sunglasses from his face. "Pretty sharp for government issue."

The spook began to make a move, then checked himself. He stood blinking at Cox, not quite knowing how to proceed. The field manuals had not covered this particular contingency.

"Are you Colonel Daniel Cox?" the second spook repeated.

"No, sir, I'm Raniel Dox," he returned. "You must want my smarter, and better-looking, younger brother. Get out your pencils and I'll give you two sharp dressers his phone number."

"Damn it, Cox," the second Company man shouted, balling his fists, "this is no laughing matter, but you must reply in the affirmative for us to continue. There are certain new protocols."

"Protocols, huh?" Cox exclaimed, having grown tired of baiting the two field assets. "Well, I've got a few of my own. Such as wanting to know on what authority you've sought me out."

One of the two men flipped open his wallet and Cox saw the CIA ID with the man's picture next to a number without a name behind the half-toned image of the CIA seal: the head of a bald eagle surmounting a shield containing a compass rose above the slogan "And ye shall know the truth and the truth shall make you free."

"Okay, you got me," Cox acknowledged as he scanned the card. "Colonel Dan Cox, retired, at your service."

"Is there somewhere we can talk?" the two men asked Cox. "Somewhere away from the crowd?"

Cox considered for a moment whether he wanted to talk to the spooks or not. He had stayed with the SR surveillance program until the bitter end, right up until May of 1990, when the final Blackbird recon aircraft had been turned into a museum piece by the Air Force, which had flown them for the Company.

There was no place left for him, a cold warrior at heart, after Congress and high operating costs had quashed the program forever. On being awarded the Company's Silver Retirement Medallion—a "jockstrap medal," so named because it was not to be displayed in public—Cox had gone to Bali.

For the past two years he had tried hard to forget all about his former life.

"Over this way," he told the spooks after a short pause during which his curiosity had managed to get the best of him.

Cox brought the two men over to the edge of the crowd. They stood together on the perimeter of the palm grove and Cox let them make their pitch.

"What we're about to tell you is subject to the amended FOIA Security Act of 1984," the first one began. "Do you hereby swear never to disclose the substance of the discussion we are about to have?"

"So help me God," Cox replied mockingly. "Get on with it."

"Your country needs you, Cox," the second "bluesuiter" said, his deadpan expression unchanged. "Our intelligence satellites are being blinded by some unknown force. We need you to perform one final mission. We want you to overfly a section of Russia with a retrofitted Blackbird and bring back the data that's critical to our national security."

"Well, I can give you a definite maybe on that, guys," Cox told the Company assets, preparing to leave. "Now, if you'll excuse me . . ."

"We need to know *now,*" the first Company man told Cox. "There isn't time to wait for your answer."

"Damn you shitheads!" Cox shouted. "You turn me into a dinosaur, tell me I'm obsolete, put me out to pasture, and then you think you can walk right into my life and drag me away to do 'one last mission.' Just who the hell do you think you are anyway?"

"Look, Cox," the second CIA man put in, laying a hand on his shoulder. "If it's any consolation, we don't blame you for the way you feel. But you're the only individual who can perform the mission. There isn't time to train another pilot to do the job. The other pilots on our list simply don't have your experience flying the SR-71. We'll leave you alone if you decline, but the man we chose might not measure up to the demands made on him."

Cox shook off his hand in exasperation and walked back toward the ceremonial cremation platform. Before he had gone more than a few paces, he stopped and turned toward the two Company messengers.

"I'll do it, you bastards," he said. Again he began walking toward the sacred grove. Then, suddenly remembering something, Cox spun around. "I forgot to give you back your shades," he said with a smile.

Moscow

Russian President Sergei Pavlovich looked out the window of his office in the Kremlin. Sleet fell in thick sheets. Several stories below, Red Square was filled with scurrying black figures, many under the canopies of open umbrellas. The Motherland had its share of problems, but the Russian leader had been unnerved by the U.S. President's call.

There was no doubt that a serious threat faced the Commonwealth. One far more serious than the recent coup attempt. In truth, he had feared something of its nature materializing.

Picking his way carefully through the snake pit of intrigues which daily threatened to smash the fragile relationship of ethnic republics asunder had made sleep impossible for many months. In such an atmosphere the unthinkable was always the first possibility to be considered.

However, the implications of what he knew to be true were nothing short of staggering. These ominous new rumblings from hard-liners could plunge the entire world into chaos. Something had to be done, and done soon, or catastrophe was virtually assured.

The buzzing of his intercom took President Pavlovich from his vigil at the moisture-streaked window. His secretary informed him that Valery Samsonov had arrived and was awaiting him in the office vestibule.

"Good," Pavlovich said into the intercom. "Send him right in."

Samsonov was a short, nondescript-looking man with a face resembling that of a small, rodent-hunting mammal, habitually attired in a rumpled suit.

He was also the Director of the Komitet Gosudarstvennoy Bezopastnosti, the Committee for State Security, more commonly known by its initials: KGB; and he possessed one of the keenest analytical minds since Lavrenty Beria.

Samsonov and the Russian leader went back to the early days of the post-Stalin era. They had begun their service in the KGB together during the Khrushchev era had lived through the dark days of the Cuban missile crisis, a time which had impressed upon them both the need for a policy of nuclear cutbacks.

One of Pavlovich's first acts since the collapse of the Moscow political machine, or Mossoviet, had been to appoint Samsonov as the director of the Komitet when that post had become vacant upon the suicide of the legendary spymaster Nemekov for his treasonous actions in supporting the junta members.

The appointment had appeased intelligence hard-liners, who saw this as a signal that the KGB's powers were to be expanded, while at the same time mollifying those factions that believed Russian intelligence needed to benefit from the same technology that the Americans were famous for deploying.

But to Pavlovich, the Samsonov appointment meant that he would have a direct window on the inner workings of the KGB and, therefore, a source of great power enjoyed by few of his predecessors since Stalin himself.

The President pulled aside a bookcase and ushered Samsonov into a special room. Its walls were copper-clad to be impermeable to all known forms of electronic bugging. It had no windows that could be scanned by lasers that picked up the faint vibrations on glass caused by the human voice and amplified them for recording.

The room was regularly swept for bugs twice each day. In its bugproof confines, the Russian President could speak frankly with Samsonov without fear of being overheard.

"The news is not good, Sergei Grigor'ch," Samsonov told the Premier. "I have done as you instructed. I have made discreet inquiries through trustworthy channels. My inquiries have revealed some disquieting facts."

The Premier watched Samsonov, stroking his chin.

"Go on," he said.

"There seem to be discrepancies in the number of systems reported in the order of battle," the KGB director began. "Specifically, there are three Blackjack long-range bombers presently unaccounted for. We do not know the locations of these planes, which are equipped with AS-15 long-range nuclear cruise missiles. That is the worst of it. There are sizable quantities of other war materiel unaccounted for as well."

From his briefcase Samsonov took a sheaf of computer printouts stapled together and laid them atop the desk separating him from the President.

"This is the complete manifest," he said. "From what I have been able to ascertain, it covers a period dating back over the last two years."

"How could this have happened?" the President asked, already knowing that it was a naive question.

"Very simple, actually," Samsonov responded, his features as always devoid of expression. *"Gol na vydumki khitra*—'the naked have sly devices.' In our efforts to evade complete compliance with Start, we have resorted to undercounting and moving our war materiel around.

"Such a policy could permit commanders at high echelons to bring off similar diversionary measures, differing only insofar as they serve to consolidate their own power rather than the good of Russia."

"Do you have names?" the President asked, remembering that it was he who had readily agreed to the deception. It had seemed like a good idea at the time: holding the whip hand, the Americans had forced his side to make concessions which would leave the U.S. with far fewer warheads but still give them a clear tactical nuclear superiority.

In a world where today's friends could quickly become tomorrow's enemies, such a posture was not deemed desirable and would never had been agreed to if it were not for the Rodina's present dire problems. When the Soviet Union had been stronger, similar cuts proposed in President Carter's SALT Treaty were unilaterally turned down.

"No names yet," Samsonov replied, shaking his head. "However, I suspect the northern Russian Republic to be the ultimate destination of the aircraft. Only in an area as large as that could there be any chance of hiding such heavy bombers successfully."

"We must nip this matter in the bud," the President said, standing and pacing the bugproof room. "But not through channels. The matter must be handled with speed and silence. It must be as though it had never happened. To do otherwise would be to admit that I have utterly lost control over the nation.

"At present the Americans still support a centrally governed Commonwealth. To show them that this arrangement is but a fiction would be an admission that our adversaries are correct and an even more divided and weakened nation better serves their strategic ends."

"I understand perfectly," Samsonov told the President. "And I have the following recommendation to make: deploy a small force of elite commandos. Let them recce the area and, when they find the base, destroy it utterly."

"But who?" asked the President.

"There is one man who can do the job," Samsonov answered. "Boris Mikhailovich Tallin."

"Tallin?" the Premier mused, trying to place the name, then suddenly remembering. "But Tallin is in Lefortovo, isn't he?"

Samsonov nodded. "Correct," he acknowledged. "But his sentence can be commuted at your discretion. And I can state with full confidence that there is no better man suited to this undertaking than Boris Mikhail'ch. After all, were not the 'criminal' acts which Tallin committed precisely those which we wish performed now, albeit in the name of national security?"

For the first time since the start of the secret briefing, Samsonov saw President Pavlovich smile and begin to show signs of relaxing.

"Of course," he told Samsonov in a moment. "Tallin is our man. Why had I not thought of it myself?"

5

Lomax, Virginia

The Defense Advanced Research Programs Agency (DARPA) was responsible for carrying out the research and development which went into producing ongoing generations of weapons for the U.S. military.

In a post-Cold War era of chronically shrinking budgets, coupled with an astronomical upward spiral in cost overruns incurred in the deployment of major weapons systems, one of DARPA's priorities for some years had been to design and construct ever more sophisticated training simulators.

DARPA's Lomax facility was a complex of unobtrusive concrete blockhouses, barracks buildings and inflatable Quonset-type structures. Their lack of architectural personality belied the fact that some of the most advanced weapons systems research and development projects were undertaken inside them.

Located underground within a complex of enormous concrete bunkers was what base insiders had christened The Arcade. It was where work on the most closely guarded of DARPA's secret projects was performed.

In one such bunker, Dan Cox was to begin a crash course in training for the mission that by now had received the code name Watchtower.

Leo Applegate, systems manager for the training facility, greeted Cox topside on his arrival at the facility's main building at ground level, where he received a clip-on ID tag from the security desk officer, who had phoned Applegate and informed him that Cox had just arrived on base.

Applegate, a goateed man of middle age with twin-kling gray eyes that communicated the merriment of a child set loose in a toy department and a spearpoint of thinning hair brushed back from an otherwise pink bald skull, had been one of the past champions of simulator technology. He had insisted since the fifties that simu-lators could save lives and make deploying weapons systems in the field both more efficient and cost-effective. Time and evaporating military budgets had borne Applegate out in this claim.

Applegate was taking a bite out of what looked like a ham sandwich on seedless rye as he walked toward Cox.

"Howdy," Applegate told Cox, extending his hand. He felt Cox's firm, dry grip as he held the bitten-on sandwich in his other hand. "The elevator's right over here. Let's ride down," he said, already ushering Cox toward the door with the eagerness of a kid wanting to show a playmate his newest toy. "Unless you want something to eat first?"

"No, thanks," Cox told Applegate. "I'm okay."

"Fine, but I gotta tell you, we've got some pretty darn good blueberry pie over at the commissary," he went on, taking another bite out of the ham sandwich.

"No, thanks," Cox repeated with a half smile. "I'm really fine."

"Great," Applegate replied. "Didn't mean to pressure you."

He punched the floor button and the elevator began its descent, stopping a few minutes later at another level of the underground base while Applegate stuffed more ham and rye bread into his mouth.

When the doors opened, Cox had to suppress the urge to let out a long whistle of astonishment. The elevator had deposited them on the ground level of an enormous chamber with a cathedral-height ceiling.

Set high on its walls were the longitudinal bubbles of Plexiglas viewing chambers.

Arrayed throughout the chamber was an assortment of simulator machines which could duplicate the entire gamut of air, land and sea tactical situations in any kind of military hardware. Of various configurations and sizes, their exteriors glinted dully under the glare of overhead lights.

Applegate sensed Cox's initial reaction; it was common for first-time visitors to be overwhelmed by the scope of what they saw. He smiled and said, "Grabs you, don't it? If I do say so myself, we're pretty proud of The Arcade. We can damn near simulate any combat situation you can imagine on any piece of hardware you can name, from the B-2 bomber to the M-1 Abrams. How long has it been since you've done any qual-sim time?"

"Not since '88 or thereabouts," Cox replied, his voice echoing in the vast, concrete-walled chamber as they walked together into the center of the simulator training facility.

"Hell, that's practically the Stone Age," Applegate commented with a laugh, then crammed the last piece of ham sandwich into his mouth and chewed contemplatively before adding, "I can promise you what we have in store will knock your socks off."

Cox walked toward Simulator A, its boxlike twenty-by-ten-foot cab raised ten feet off the concrete floor of the chamber on hydraulically controlled actuators and swivel arms.

As the simulator's cab began to descend at a command from the control booth above him, where Applegate sat at the master console, Cox prepared to climb into the box, already feeling the heat building inside the air-conditioned, pressured flight suit worn in the SR's cockpit.

It was a familiar feeling, although one he had not experienced in several long years.

The flight suit was a survival necessity in the cockpit of the SR-71, which routinely cruised at the near edge of space at multi-Mach speeds. Ovenlike skin temperatures in excess of six hundred degrees Fahrenheit were normally generated during the course of an SR recon mission—twice the heat at which a cake bakes.

Such was the level of heat energy generated by the Blackbird as it arrowed through the sky at over twice the speed of a .38 caliber bullet, that pilots who touched the inch-thick Plexiglas cockpit windscreen had reported that any loose fibers of their thermally insulated gloves would begin to smoke from even a moment's brief contact and that food tubes could be heated by holding them against the glass.

The simulator cab was lowered and Cox climbed through the door, latching it closed behind him.

The interior of the simulator was both familiar and unfamiliar. Familiar because its dimensions resembled those of the Blackbird's cramped cockpit. Unfamiliar because the advanced-looking avionics surrounding him were not even remotely like those which Cox recalled from his years with the SR-71 program and which had remained virtually unchanged on the fleet of SRs for almost twenty-five years.

Once harnessed down into the pilot's chair, Cox

heard Applegate's voice crackling over his helmet comlink.

When—and if—the mission began in earnest, Cox would be flying with a reconnaissance systems officer—an RSO—in the cockpit behind his.

However, Applegate had explained that since no pilot had as yet been selected to act as Cox's backseater, he would begin training on the flight simulator individually. Applegate would play the role of RSO by remote control, and the simulator system's sophisticated computers would take care of the rest.

"I'm going to turn on the SR's avionics systems now," Applegate apprised Cox. A moment later, as if by magic, the darkened interior of the simulator cab was completely transformed.

Cox was now staring straight ahead, through the two inverted triangles of heat-resistant glass which formed the cockpit windscreens of an SR-71A Blackbird.

Outside this virtual cockpit, there stretched the black tarmac of a runway, cordoned by hundreds of tiny marker lights. Above the runway was a black, star-flecked night sky.

The computer visuals were awesome, Cox thought. They were not the blocky, low-resolution computer graphics he had expected to be confronted with during the simulator run. On the contrary, the simulated takeoff environment was eerily close to real life.

"How do you like our little magic lantern show?" Applegate asked, though from the tone of pride in his voice it was evident to Cox that he already knew the answer.

"I'm floored, App," Cox said appreciatively.

"Yeah, well, you ought to be," Applegate asserted. "The display incorporates the latest in artificial intelligence software drivers and image-processing hardware. I'm talking quadputers, here, the same technology Hollywood uses to create those three-D special effects. Only our equipment makes theirs look like kids' toys. What you are looking at is what's known around here as 'Sir TV.' That's a corruption of SRTV, or simulated real-time video. But hold onto your hat, you ain't seen nothing yet."

Before Cox would get "airborne," however, Applegate briefed him on the retrofitted avionics systems of the SR-71 that he would be flying on the mission.

In fact, as far as today went, Cox was to get a feel for the new command-and-control array, which was significantly different from the original SR-71's cockpit console, or from anything else he'd ever seen, for that matter.

In only a short time, the DARPA techs had crammed the newly retrofitted spyplane full of state-of-the-art gear, much of it cannibalized from the spanking new equipment on the slower but more cost-effective TR-1 spyplane fleet still in service with NATO.

The most immediately noticeable of these retrofittings to the SR was the main tactical scope empaneled between the main control console and the forward windscreen, the video display unit which superimposed mission data in the form of icons over the pilot's field of a system of computer-linked radars.

The next was the four nondedicated tactical VDTs, two located to each side of Cox on the instrumentation panels. The video display terminals, each one capable of displaying enhanced color graphics, would provide Cox with multimode data on what he might be facing in the air as well as what he was overflying on the ground.

The VDTs would also give him a bird's-eye view of something else entirely new.

This was the Blackbird's sole item of armament: an optomechanically guided, air-launched cruise missile.

The ALCM, a converted Maverick missile christened the Highwire, could be launched from an internal weapon bay (IWB) in the SR-71's underbelly.

The first test firing of a missile from the SR's predecessor, the A-12, had led to an AIM-7A missile being successfully deployed.

Since that time, several of the Blackbird photoreconnaissance aircraft had been equipped with at least a single AIM-7A—the same missile more commonly known as the Sparrow and carried by F15E Strike Eagles—as standard armament.

But the cruise missile which Cox could fire in case of emergency was a far more sophisticated weapon than even these weapons. A precision-guided munition with a solid track record, the Maverick had had recent modifications made to it just prior to Desert Storm that had further enhanced the round's capabilities.

As the inheritor of this technology, the Highwire terminally guided munition was equipped with an advanced anti-jamming warhead and high-lethality terminal ballistics properties that made it far deadlier than the AIM-7A or the Maverick combined.

Additionally, the ALCM could be guided directly from the SR's cockpit, its nose-mounted TV camera providing Cox with a real-time video image of breaking target data.

There was more about the ALCM that was entirely new as well.

The Highwire cruise missile's warhead contained a shaped charge of an advanced high-energy explosive, an explosive compound so powerful that its blast yield was equal to a subkiloton nuclear bomb, yet without a nuke's drawback of releasing harmful radiation into the environment. Over-the-horizon radar could guide the Highwire, which made it a fully capable stand off weapon.

"Now let's get down to the nitty-gritty," Applegate said, after he'd walked Cox through the retrofitting specs of the veteran spy aircraft. "We've got a lot of ground to cover." He unwrapped a candy bar, turned his attention to the sim console and got down to work.

6

The DIRNSA and DCI sat across from the President in the National Security Council's secure briefing room. Established by the National Security Act of 1947, the NSC is tasked with advising the President on intelligence and counterintelligence activities relating to national security.

Located in the vast underground bunker complex which stretched beneath the foundations of the White House and in which all high-level briefings were routinely conducted, it relegated the Oval Office to little more than a setting for photo opportunities rather than the site of genuine strategic planning.

The issue at hand: another orbital blinding, this one of a Rhyolite-class radar surveillance satellite.

DCI Bill Farragutt took the floor. At a signal from the Company director, the briefing room's overhead lights were dimmed. Farragutt had brought his audiovisuals with him: the large flat digital screen came to life as the VCR shunted into standby mode.

"What you are about to see, gentlemen," the DCI began, "Is video footage shot by the crew of the space shuttle *Raleigh* during its last covert mission. We had hoped to obtain some evidence of what was happening in space, some confirmation of the mechanism by which disabling was effected, and we now believe we have it."

Stepping back to one side of the large, high-definition screen, the DCI hit the play button on his hand-held remote and the VCR began rolling. The images themselves were prefaced by the opening credits, superimposed above the official CIA seal, which proclaimed that the visuals being shown were top-secret, Umbra-coded, and that copying or even divulging their contents was a serious violation of federal law.

These caveats having been dispensed with, the video footage began in earnest with a view from the space shuttle's boom-mounted cargo bay camera of an astronaut going EVA, holding what appeared to be a bulky black device in his hands that might have been a camera. As if in confirmation of this, the footage then segued into shots taken from the astronaut's point of view.

Here the visuals came to the heart meat.

The wide-angle shot depicted a cluster of weightless metal debris glinting like diamond ore as the floating particles caught the rays of the sun. The video's focus shifted, this time to another astronaut, who was gathering up the bits of metal and placing them in collection netting for retrieval.

The DCI froze the frame and stood in front of the hundred-inch video screen.

"Gentlemen," he said, "what you see here are the remains of the final Rhyolite intelligence satellite destroyed by means of what we believe is a sophisticated ground-based laser."

There was a buzz from those seated at the table in the darkness of the conference room. The DCI had been prepared for a reaction of this type. He hit the play button again and the scene shifted to footage of the retrieved fragments of the destroyed satellite now being displayed on a lab table.

The DCI zapped the image again and took a laser pointer from his top coat pocket, shooting the ruby beam at the screen and moving its small red dot to describe the outline of the largest of several metal shards shown on the screen.

"The techs tell me that this kind of flash melting pattern is characteristic of a metal envelope subjected to the stresses of rapid and intense heating of internal components. Such flash melting can only be produced by a single means: high-energy laser radiation. It's virtually a fingerprint of the technology as possible."

It was NSA Director Justin Slattery who spoke next.

"We've had some indication that the Russians were in the final stages of fielding an advanced mobile laser system, but we had no idea it was anything but disinformation."

"It's not disinformation, Justin," the DCI responded. "I don't have to tell any of you here that the Russians have been conducting advanced experiments in military lasers since the sixties. They had their first operational ground-based station by 1979 at the directed-energy-R-and-D site at Shary Sagan in Soviet Central Asia. Another watershed was reached in 1988 with the development of an accurate aiming system which could effectively compensate for atmospheric distortion. Apparently they have indeed fielded mobile laser units."

"Nothing to legally prevent them," Conrad Lowell, the Secretary of Defense, commented. "The Start Treaty doesn't expressly forbid ground-based ABM systems. If it did, we'd have to scrap Patriot."

"Correct. It does not," the DCI, turning to Lowell, amplified. "However, what we evidently are witnessing now is a deliberate attempt to blind and/or disable our intelligence-gathering platforms in space—an offensive move by anybody's yardstick."

"To what end?" asked the President, who had been listening and watching carefully. "Do we have any direct evidence that the Russians are planning some new military push?"

"Negative," the DCI replied. "Nothing as yet. But we can't rule that out. Central Intelligence does, however, believe that whatever is going on is proceeding without the direct knowledge of President Pavlovich. Despite recent purges, the data indicate the Russian military is highly factionalized. The CIA's reading of the circumstances is that a rogue commander may be behind this offensive. Nevertheless, and regardless of who is to blame, the situation is critical in its potential for rapid destabilization."

The President digested what he had just heard. The DCI's assessment confirmed his worst fears regarding a nuclear first strike from rogue forces of the former Soviet Union, fears which, paradoxically, would have been less pronounced when the U.S.S.R's highly centralized "top-down" method of nuclear control was in force.

Bancroft had still not forgotten the fact that for three days during the Kremlin coup, the Russian President had no longer controlled his nation's nuclear launch codes. Bancroft felt that he had no choice left to him now. He would immediately issue the order that the Defcon alert status be elevated from five, which constituted peacetime, to four, indicating a state of national emergency.

Defcon level one, also known as "cocked pistol," was the final Defense Readiness Condition and constituted a state of maximum-force readiness.

"I want up-to-the-minute briefings," Bancroft told the officials seated at the briefing room table. He checked his watch and continued. "I have to be at Andrews in half an hour. Keep me informed."

It was White House Press Secretary George Freeman who spoke up as the President shuffled together the papers in front of him, clearly preparing to leave the assemblage.

"How do you want me to play it?" he asked the President.

"Stonewall 'em," the President told Freeman.

Bancroft quickly exited the room, weighed down by horrifying thoughts as his Secret Service escort accompanied him to the White House's underground garage, where his executive limo waited to whisk him off to Andrews.

Lomax, Virginia

Cox had spent the final three days of his stay at the DARPA base undergoing training in the advanced flight simulator.

He had come to hate the contraption. Its audiovisuals were so real that it was almost like entering a gigantic video game. No wonder the techs at the base had nicknamed the simulator complex The Arcade.

Applegate had insisted that the technology was nowhere near mature. In a few years, cybernetic chambers would be in place to transport trainees into a virtual-reality universe in which their situational awareness would be identical to that experienced in actual combat missions. They would even be able to feel themselves die.

Cox was having some of the blueberry pie in the base commissary with Applegate—the pie was indeed as good as Applegate had promised—when a soldier came over to the table, saluted and handed Cox a sealed envelope. Cox scanned the message slip inside and handed it to Applegate.

"I see they've made it official," Applegate said after he had scanned the orders and handed them back. "Congratulations, Cox. The mission's a go."

7

Lefortovo Prison is a massive, ancient building with gray stone walls that stands in the heart of Moscow, a fortress left over from the time of Czar Nicholas the Second. It is the same prison in which West German aviator Mattias Rust was incarcerated when he was found guilty of espionage by a Soviet court after landing a light monoplane in Red Square.

Lefortovo, like all ex-Soviet prisons, including those labor camps that had been erected in the gulags of Siberia, and of which a few still remain, is a place where Soviet citizens were brought in order to be forgotten.

It is rare that prison inmates are graced with visitors, let alone visitors who are high-ranking officials of the Russian Congress of Peoples Deputies. Yet this was precisely the case for Boris Tallin one day during the twenty-second month of his five-year prison term.

A heavy snow was falling as the black Volga limousine pulled up in front of Lefortovo's imposing gates and the official got out and walked crisply up to the security desk in the cavernous lobby of the prison's main building. The official presented his security pass and asked to see Tallin at once. He was soon admitted to the prison cellblock where Tallin was incarcerated.

The narrow corridor was long and tunnellike. Its

walls were painted an institutional cream-on-green and the corridor was dimly illuminated by wire-caged light bulbs spaced at five-foot intervals in the ceiling. The cramped passsageway smelled mustily of dry rot and had thick bunches of pipes carrying electrical cables running along its length.

Along the sides of the walls of this particular cell-block, which was reserved for those convicted of crimes against the state, were doors of heavy iron, each with a judas hole set in its face through which food could be passed and jailers could look in on the prisoners at any time of the day or night.

Inside the third door on the right from where the corridor began was Boris Tallin. He was playing Tetris on a small Japanese-made video game approximately the size of a cigarette pack. Tallin had become addicted to the electronic games while in prison. They challenged his mind and helped him to pass the time.

"Here is the prisoner's cell," the block warden said to Samsonov, stopping before the door and selecting from the iron ring on his belt the large latchkey which fit into the primitive lock. He proceeded to rap on the door, then pulled aside the judas hole. "Boris Mikhail'ch Tallin," he announced into the cell. "You have a visitor."

"Tell whoever it is to get fucked," Tallin shouted back, and those in the corridor could hear the faint pings and bleeps of the video game he played as he lay on his bunk. "I'm busy."

"Watch your foul mouth," the cell commander ordered angrily. "Your visitor is Committee for State Security Chairman Samsonov."

"Then tell the bastard to get doubly fucked," Tallin roared from his cell. "Communism is dead and the KGB is even deader."

Samsonov headed off the cellblock warden before he

could say or do any more, saying, "Let me speak with him, please."

The block warden unlocked the door of the cell and Samsonov stood in the doorway. Tallin looked up at the KGB chief with a scowl on his hard, angular face.

He recognized Samsonov only too well.

It had been Samsonov, after all, who had been instrumental in his rotting away in Lefortovo for the past year and ten months—Samsonov and the rest of the former Politburo bigwigs who had conspired to make Tallin disappear into the dehumanizing machinery of one of the worst prisons in the world.

Tallin put away his Japanese video game and sat up on the edge of the bed.

"It has been a long time, Boris Mikhail'ch," Samsonov said to Tallin, noting that the time spent in prison had not seemed to have harmed the former Spetsnaz commando.

His angular face was leanly chiseled and the biceps which showed through the A-shirt he wore were massively sinewed. The presence of exercise equipment in the narrow cell attested to Samsonov that Tallin was not allowing himself to go to seed while in prison. That was all to the good, thought Samsonov to himself.

"Not too long to suit me, Samsonov," Tallin replied gruffly. "You and those bastards in the GRU have a lot to answer for. I should beat the shit out of you right now, if you want the truth. I could probably get in a few good licks before they stopped me."

Samsonov gestured for the guard to shut the door and told him he would be okay. The guard, eying the prisoner with skepticism and disdain, told Samsonov that he would be waiting right outside, ready to intervene if Tallin tried anything. Samsonov thanked the guard for his concern and walked over to Tallin, unafraid of the powerful man's blustering threats.

"You were given a fair trial and were found guilty," Samsonov began. "The acts you committed were treasonous breaches of national security."

"What I did was an act of patriotism, you sanctimonious idiot! And you damned well know it!" Tallin shouted. "In the past year, in fact, the GRU has plugged those very leaks that I proved existed. And for my thanks I get thrown away to deteriorate in this shithole."

Samsonov knew that what Tallin had told him was true. A Spetsnaz commando veteran in Afghanistan, he had distinguished himself above all others and had earned a chestful of combat decorations, some of which were for bravery under fire during an episode in the mountains near Kabul which was still a classified military matter.

Upon his return from the war zone, Tallin had not sat idly waiting to collect his veteran's pension benefits. He had immediately taken up a cause which he deemed vital to the national interest.

The state of Soviet military security was atrocious, he had claimed. Soviet bases could be breached easily by the Americans or anyone else with minimal special operations expertise coupled with the will to use it. With almost fanatical zeal, Tallin had set out to prove his assertions correct.

Gathering together a cadre of former Spetsnaz commandos with whom he had served in Afghanistan, Tallin created a group which he code-named Bear's Claw. The mission of this commando unit was to attempt to infiltrate Soviet military bases, thus identifying the weak points in their security systems.

In the end, Tallin's efforts had proved too successful for his own good. On virtually every attempt, Tallin's group of commandos had been able to breach the security of their target bases.

Had Bear's Claw chosen to adopt and maintain a lower profile, it might have gone better for its leader. But Tallin had opted instead to trumpet his successes in the open media, thereby exposing the weakness of the system in a glaring light.

He had made enemies by the score.

Powerful enemies.

"You are here today, Boris Mikhail'ch," Samsonov told the prisoner, "because you dared to say what others only thought and because you did not fear to tread on any toes by doing so. In the process you embarrassed powerful men.

"Perhaps you don't realize it, but I am your friend. There were those who would have preferred that you be executed for treason. I argued otherwise. Serving your time even here at Lefortovo is better than what might have otherwise befallen you."

Tallin was silent, thinking back upon his time spent here behind bars: wasted years which the Party had robbed him of forever, years which he would never be able to get back. Presently he turned and looked at the emissary from the Center through gimlet eyes.

From the beginning it had been obvious that the ex-commando would be offered a deal of some kind. The new Chairman of the KGB had not come to shoot the breeze with one of Lefortovo's most infamous prisoners.

Something big, Tallin knew, was in the offing.

Some matter of vast importance and great urgency had come up, requiring skills that only he possessed, or he would never have been contacted.

And now Tallin was going to hear all about it.

"I am prepared to offer you a full pardon," Samsonov stated, "in return for using your martial skills on behalf of our beloved Rodina."

As Tallin listened, Samsonov told him more details

about the nature of the mission which he would undertake.

Tallin began to smile.

For the first time in a very long while, life held promise again.

8

The hangar's location was Umbra-coded.

Excavated from beneath the desert sands as part of a vast subterranean military installation complex, it took up the same space as three gymnasiums set end to end and was hardened against a near miss by nuclear warheads. Unofficially, it was known as the Black Hole.

The hangar was used by the CIA, the NSA and the Air Force to house their most secret military projects. Stealth bombers had been deployed here while undergoing post-roll-out testing, but today an aircraft which had been mothballed before the secret facility had ever been completed stood gleaming dully beneath the overhead lights as the technical support crew made last-minute alterations to its sleek black airframe.

The SR-71A Blackbird stood in the center of the hangar, a winged black dagger whose special radar-absorbent "blackball" paint job seemed to draw light into the plane, making it look like a machine constructed out of the very stuff of shadows. The SR bore no markings save for small red serial numbers on the inside of each vertical tail surface.

A smooth, tapering chine extended from the plane's nose assembly out to the sides of the SR's fuselage and two double delta wings, each blended with the bulging nacelles of the spyplane's twin turbo ramjet Pratt & Whitney engines.

The needle-ended cones of electro-hydraulically actuated translating intake spikes protruded from each nacelle; at supersonic velocities air pressure would force them down into the engine shock traps of the SR to "shock down" air passing across them for a more burnable fuel mixture. Each engine was capable of burning eighty thousand gallons of fuel per hour and producing thirty-two thousand five hundred pounds of thrust, and was so powerful that at Mach two it generated only 17.6 percent of total thrust capacity.

Viewed from the front, the Blackbird resembled the embodiment of secrecy and stealth. Its clean lines, fooling the eye into seeing an almost disklike shape, unmistakably identified the aircraft as a tool of covert intelligence. Viewed from the rear, the louvered nozzle vanes of the Blackbird's engine nacelles bespoke the power which the sleek black sky ship held latent within her chined delta airframe.

Dan Cox, wearing his flight suit, walked from the ready room in which he had been receiving a last-minute briefing from mission control manager Martin Holloway, the same Holloway who had flown as his RSO years before. Unlike Cox, Holloway had opted to trade his cockpit for a desk at Langley.

As he saw the Blackbird crouched in the distance like an enormous metal raven on her three titanium-cast landing gear, Cox felt butterflies in the stomach of a kind which he had not experienced since his days as a rookie pilot.

Now, once again, Cox was a rookie of sorts. The retrofitted spyplane was newer, faster, stealthier and more mission-capable than it had ever been before.

The Blackbird had been improved in every conceivable manner during the short space of time the techs had been given to prepare it for the mission. From its avionics and ergonomics to the more lightweight pressure suits that its pilots would wear throughout the upcoming mission flights, the SR had been completely overhauled.

Cox knew that he was about to fly a perfect blend between a proven jet aircraft and the end product of the latest in military electronics and aeronautics.

In the same tradition of rapid design and deployment that had produced the original SR in only twenty-six months after program approval, retrofittings had been made to the SR. The techs had practically reinvented the wheel.

The upcoming flight would only be a dry run before the final go order was given—the mission might yet be aborted at this point, although this did not appear likely—but it would not be a mere simulator exercise Cox would be undertaking.

He would be *flying,* using the new equipment retrofitted into the Blackbird.

But where was his RSO? Cox wondered. Holloway had told Cox that the reconnaissance systems operator selected for the mission was being trained separately and that Cox would meet his backseater just before boarding the aircraft.

In the interim, Cox went over to the plane. There he stood watching the ground crew filling the SR-71's tanks with JP-7 aviation fuel—tanks which included its revolutionary "wet wings"—and the B7 starter cart unit which was attached to the SR via cables to prime its engines.

Below, on the underbelly of the craft, the techs were installing the sophisticated ELINT and photosurveillance pods whose data would be instantly digitized by the small yet powerful computers carried onboard.

In the old days, an SR-71 mission would have its

collected intelligence data recorded on computer tape and the visuals stored in the form of exposed film to be developed back at Meade. That was an era in which film packets were dropped from satellites, rather than beamed down in the form of coded telemetry.

Now, thousands of times more data would be stored on a single compact disk which, if necessary, could be accessed directly from the cockpit instrumentation panel by the pilot or the RSO, who would enjoy almost full interchangeability of mission roles if and when the need arose.

As he observed the ground crew ministering to the SR, Cox was suddenly aware that Holloway had come over and had begun to say something to him.

"Recognize the serial number?" he asked.

Cox had, and looked again at the numerals: 17974 in red on the inner surface of one of the SR's vertical stabilizers, designating one of the most famous planes in aviation history.

"Ichi Ban," Cox said.

"That's right," Holloway returned. "Flew nearly sixty covert missions before being retired to Beale. But she's still the best plane in the fleet, better now that we've refitted her. Anyway," Holloway went on, "there's somebody I want you to meet. It's your RSO."

Cox turned and looked at the RSO and was startled by the diminutive person wearing a flight suit that seemed overly large for the flier's frame.

The RSO was a woman.

As if seeing the shock reflected on Cox's suddenly livid face, Holloway quickly made his introductions.

"Lieutenant Amanda Gilroy," he said, "I'd like you to meet the man you'll be flying this mission alongside, Colonel Dan Cox."

Gilroy, a pretty blond woman who could not be past her mid-twenties, extended her gloved hand to Cox.

"Glad to meet you, Colonel," she said with a smile. "I'm looking forward to the mission."

Cox shook Gilroy's hand, trying hard to conceal the conflicting emotions he felt, emotions which ran the gamut from mortification to a ridiculous mirth born of being confronted by what he considered to be the ultimate absurdity.

Though he kept his face deadpanned, Cox flashed a telling look at Holloway, who caught Cox's meaning and shrugged in wordless response, as if to say, "Don't blame me, I only work here."

"Excuse me, Lieutenant," Cox told Gilroy after shaking the blond woman's hand. "I'd like to have a word in private with Holloway if I may."

"Sure thing," she said cheerfully, but Cox already had his arm around Holloway's neck in a none-too-brotherly manner and was steering him to a portion of the underground hangar out of earshot of the ground crew.

"You sonofabitch!" Cox snarled at Holloway. "You knew about this all along, didn't you?"

"It was a last-minute assignment," Holloway pleaded defensively. "We couldn't find anyone with the right qualifications who wouldn't turn down the mission."

"Bullshit!" Cox roared. "You knew my RSO was going to be a woman all along. You deliberately kept that information from me. Tell me the truth, you miserable, lying spook-fucker."

"Keep your voice down," Holloway responded, afraid Cox was about to turn violent on him, a legitimate enough concern given Cox's reputation as a brawler. "All right. We didn't know . . . I mean, you're known as kind of a white buffalo type to a lot of people in intelligence. We had Gilroy on tap from the first— believe me, Dan, she's the best ELINT officer you could ask for—but we didn't know if you'd go for it."

"At least you were right about one thing," Cox told him. "I *won't* go for it. It's not that I don't think women don't have any place in the military—obviously they do. But there are some places I don't think women should be, and one of them's in what's tantamount to a big bladder of jet fuel screaming along at over three times the speed of sound above the opposition's territory. Either you get me another RSO—one who can piss standing up, I might add—or I am out of here, bucko."

Moments later, Holloway was staring at Cox's back, his chest smarting from where Cox's fingertips had repeatedly jabbed it, as the pilot stalked away from the center of the hangar toward the ready room's door.

Cox saw a candy machine in the corner and bought himself a Little Debbie bar. He sat at the table sullenly munching the candy bar, then looked out through the room's plate-glass window and saw that Gilroy had walked over to Holloway.

"What's the matter with him?" Gilroy asked Holloway, out of earshot of Cox, who continued to munch the candy bar with a scowl on his face. "I suppose the sexist pig reacted the way you guys figured he would."

"Don't worry about Cox," Holloway told Gilroy. "He's a moody sonofabitch, but he's also the best goddamn SR-71 pilot the Air Force ever produced. He'll come around. Just hang in there."

Gilroy did just that. She hung around while Cox watched Holloway head toward the ready room from the hangar, by this time munching a second candy bar, this one a Triple Dip Gonzo.

9

Zagorsk, Russia, C.I.S.

The cluster of ramshackle buildings was what remained of an abandoned farm collective dating back to before the Brezhnev years.

Tallin had spent the past few days scouting out a possible location to train his vasaltnicki team for the mission he had accepted from Samsonov in return for the commutation of his prison sentence.

For once, luck was with him.

Tallin had found the abandoned kolkhoz in the countryside not far from the Zagorsk railway terminal.

The isolated location was perfectly suited to his operational needs.

For one thing, it was only a little over seventy-five kilometers from Moscow, which made driving to and from the training site a simple matter.

For another, the site was situated far off the beaten path, its only avenue of access a dirt farm track extending from the main road and rambling for a few hundred yards through a stretch of wooded hillside.

It had not taken Tallin long to find the three other men who would, together with himself, comprise the nucleus of the vasaltnicki team.

Piotr, Gennady and Mikhail were all easily traced through the unofficial network of Afghanistan veterans which had sprung into being in the wake of governmental apathy to the rehabilitation of returning Afghanistan war veterans.

The men had all been employed as poorly paid day laborers who, without exception, had supplemented their incomes on the black market and were anxious to take on the mission, especially when Tallin told them they would be well compensated for the risks incurred.

Now Tallin watched as his three vasaltnicki squad leaders stood firing the SMGs which Tallin had been able to procure.

They were the newest and the best weapons currently available, SITES Spectre submachine guns.

Firing the 9 mm PB rounds, the Spectres featured two extraordinary advancements over all other conventional SMGs.

The first of these advancements was the SMG's high-capacity magazines, each holding fifty rounds.

The second advancement was that the Spectre featured a double-action bolt system, which meant that it did not have to be cocked before being fired, a tremendous aid in fast-breaking tactical situations.

"Very good, Piotr," Tallin commended the oldest and most skilled of his three vasaltnickis as Piotr ran in a hard-to-hit crouch toward a line of silhouette targets, firing pulsed multiround bursts to both conserve ammunition and place the rounds accurately on target.

"The rest of you, pay attention to Piotr," Tallin added. "He's got the 'capture and move' maneuver down pat."

In addition to the Spectres, the team would also be fielding Ultimax 100 light machine guns.

The Ultimax 100 series fired the NATO caliber SS109 cartridge and, while light enough to be accurately fired with one hand, was equipped with a one-hundred-round drum magazine.

The lightweight guns favored by the American Delta Force were far superior to anything in the Russian inventory, and Tallin's familiarity with unconventional assault weapons had indicated that they would be superb weapons for the close-in yet potentially intense fighting which the mission might require the commando assault team to undergo.

Each member of the unit would also carry a full complement of hand grenades and remote-triggered antipersonnel submunitions. Night-vision equipment, also state-of-the-art, would be included in his kit as well, along with RPG-18 multiple rocket launchers to be deployed in heavy-assault situations.

As Tallin watched his men run through their paces on the covert firing range, he allowed his mind to play back the events which had transpired in the days since Samsonov's visit to his cell at Lefortovo and his subsequent release from prison.

The time had passed quickly. There had been much to do and little time in which to get everything accomplished.

That the Komitet chairman's proposition was serious was evidenced not only by the speed of Tallin's release from Lefortovo but by the fact that Tallin had received every piece of exotic military hardware he had requisitioned without protest.

There had been none of the predictable excuses, none of the expectable delays.

The consignment of weapons, ammunition, fatigue battle dress and other items of combat materiel had been delivered promptly, and the equipment manifest was faithful to Tallin's order down to the last bullet.

Because Piotr, Gennady and Mikhail had been involved with the Bear's Claw penetrations of specially targeted military installations, Tallin had little doubt that the training he envisioned for the upcoming mission would proceed smoothly and efficiently.

It did.

Though they had not been involved with any sort of military undertaking in almost two years since Bear Claw's activities had been brought to an abrupt halt, his three former commandos instantly became proficient in the handling of the new weapons they had been issued, albeit after a little rust was scraped off their long-disused talents.

Tallin had complete faith that his warriors would perform superbly in the field. However, it was the nature of the mission itself that had recently begun to trouble him.

Samsonov had at first attempted to evade the necessity of giving Tallin a detailed rundown on the full parameters of the mission, citing "need to know" and using other bureaucratic double-talk to justify his evasiveness.

Finally Tallin had informed Samsonov that if he was not fully briefed on the mission, including the hazards that it might entail, then the Center could get themselves another fool to do it for them.

Backed against a wall, knowing full well that there was no other man capable of doing the job, Samsonov had been forced to reveal to Tallin the suspicions entertained by himself and the Russian President, to the effect that a rogue commander was positioning himself for a grab for political power, exploiting the restiveness of the nation to stage a new military coup d'état.

At once Tallin understood the pressing need for a well-trained, mission-capable yet compact force of rapid-strike commandos. It would have to be a force to be reckoned with, but at the same time one which could operate in the gray area of commando subwarfare beyond the normal scope of Spetsnaz activities.

If there was indeed a conspiracy to grab power from both the Center and the republics, then anything was possible and no elements of the government and military could be held above suspicion.

Still, Tallin wondered if there was not another facet to the issue of which he was still unaware, some subtle nuance which he had not been informed about and which might make him and his men pawns in a larger power game with more complex levels of depth than was apparent on the surface.

Deep inside him, he knew that this x-factor existed, if for no other reason than the fact that it was in the nature of his experience in dealing with the covert taskmasters like Samsonov that for every card they dealt, another was hidden up their sleeves.

Gorbatovo mogila ispravit, went the old Russian proverb: "only the grave straightens the hunchback."

Tallin's thoughts were broken by the beeping of his wrist chronometer, informing him that it was time to halt the automatic-weapons training exercises and take a brief break before commencing training in land-reconnaissance and escape-and-evasion techniques.

These would consume the remainder of the afternoon and the vasaltnicki's needed a well-deserved rest.

Piotr came over to Tallin as he sat on a fallen log smoking a prized American cigarette, the ones that came in the unique red-and-white packs.

Piotr was a hard-faced man with large hands and a scar running down one side of his face in the shape of a half-moon; this was the legacy of a Mujahideen dagger that had been intended for his belly many long years ago.

Piotr had saved Tallin's life in a battle some ten years before to take Sanga, a Mujahideen mountain fortress at Spin Ghar Bor in southern Afghanistan. Tallin would never forget Piotr's single-handed storming of the base, armed only with an AK-47 and a few grenades to break him out of the enemy trap.

He had also been one of the few men who had made it alive out of the Markhaz—the fortified Spetsnaz base in the Afghan mountains—during the treacherous departure of their commanding officer, a pig who had left them all there to die.

"How do you think it goes?" Piotr asked Tallin.

"It goes well," Tallin replied immediately. "You and the others are performing superbly. If I seem to be pushing you a little hard, it is only because we have very little time. The order to proceed may come to us at any moment."

Piotr was reflective as he stared across the buildings and saw Mikhail and Gennady engaging in martial arts activities, their legs and arms flailing at each other in Hwa Rang Do combat moves.

He turned to Tallin and asked him point-blank what he thought would happen to them.

"I don't know, Piotr," Tallin answered truthfully. "We are all expendable in the eyes of the Samsonovs of the world. However," he continued, "what were our lives like before this? For myself, I was in prison. Yet maybe the three of you were in a prison of sorts too."

Piotr stared up at the cloudless sky and listened to the cawing of a crow off in the trees somewhere.

He agreed with Tallin. Anything was preferable to the gray lives they had led since returning from the front. They had known the privations of combat, but also a strange, mad joy that nothing before or since had ever matched.

But it was soon time to resume the training session. The vasaltnicki team had still much ground to cover.

Soon the chattering of automatic weapons once again broke the stillness of the country afternoon, mixed with the shouts of men who were readying themselves to die.

10

Las Mesas, Nevada

A tractor vehicle hauled the SR-71 from the Black Hole's underground hangar. Fully fueled, the Blackbird held 84,180 pounds of special JP-7 aviation fuel and high-temperature sealant mixture.

Most of the interior of the spyplane's fuselage had been designed to function as a huge storage tank containing the JP-7. Literally bulging at the seams, the high-octane fuel leaked out from between the riveted plates of the aircraft's fuselage.

It would continue doing so as the SR took off and got airborne, at which point a system of centrifugal pumps would kick in, stabilizing flow patterns while the sealant additive inhibited fuel leakage. When the SR reached its multi-Mach cruising speed, the friction of its passage through the air would heat the fuel contents to a bubbling broth.

Piloting the aircraft, Dan Cox now sat in the SR's cockpit with Gilroy seated in the RSO's station behind him. Cox had grudgingly come around to accepting the female RSO but had reserved his final approval pending how well she performed on the check ride of the retrofitted aircraft.

Holloway, the mission control manager, gave Cox clearance to taxi the SR toward the runway.

Cox pulled back the spyplane's throttle and felt the entire aircraft vibrate as its two Pratt & Whitney JT11D-20B engines delivered thousands of pounds of thrust from their air-breathing turbines. Red hazard lights blinked on and off at the top and bottom of the SR's fuselage as incandescent exhaust gases shot from the Blackbird's engine nacelles into the night.

The black stealth ship began to surge forward and bounced on its landing gear for a moment. Cox felt the Blackbird give a sudden lurch, then experienced a moment of weightlessness as the landing gear left the tarmac and the sleek fuselage rose into the air.

Pushing the aircraft to the limits of its performance envelope, Cox climbed rapidly to an elevation of forty thousand feet. At that point he throttled up to the final stop and kicked the plane into full afterburner.

Immediately the Blackbird shot forward, fire streaking from its twin turbo ramjet engine nacelles in long, scorching tracks containing the characteristic "shock diamonds" in the afterburner plume.

"Let's take her through her paces," Cox said into his helmet mike.

"Roger, boss," Gilroy responded, having easily slipped into a familiar form of address to the older man, which made Cox hard put to suppress a smile each time he heard Gilroy use it.

Gilroy was scanning her multiple nondedicated screens, which relayed data from the ELINT detection blisters mounted on the spy aircraft's fuselage and from the high-definition cameras on the SR's black underbelly.

The RSO's excitement was matched only by her fear: this was to be Gilroy's first non-qual-sim flight in an SR-71, and the mission's time frame would not permit her to make another live training run.

Cox's task throughout the course of the flight would

be to push the Blackbird's performance envelope, while Gilroy would fully vet the advanced thermal imaging (TI) sensors, ground-mapping radars, low-light television (LLTV) and photomechanical systems that would be deployed during the actual mission to gather image and signals intelligence of the Russian Republic.

On this check ride, the Blackbird's flight path would take it from Las Mesas, across southern Nevada, down across Utah and Colorado and back again to base. Estimated mission time would be just under three hours.

It would be a short hop compared with any of the missions Cox had previously flown in either the SR series or its predecessor, the A-12, but it would be sufficient both to test the aircraft's performance capabilities and to give himself and Gilroy valuable hands-on experience with the Blackbird's newly revamped avionics systems.

The Blackbird handled superbly as Cox, on full afterburner thrust, tweaked the system to hand-fly the SR across the Nevada sky at constantly increasing Mach numbers. As he drove the SR, Cox felt the familiar surge of adrenaline coursing through his bloodstream, engergizing his body and infusing his mind with total clarity.

Seated behind the SR's refurbished controls, Cox knew that his situational awareness was radically different from anything he had felt during the many simulator hours he'd logged in the box.

However realistic the sim computers might have made the piloting experience, their capabilities were still a long way from duplicating the enhanced state of seeing, feeling and thinking to be gained only from actually driving the spyplane.

Going ultrasonic, Cox climbed the SR-71 even higher, arrowing toward the top of the sky. For her own part, Gilroy didn't pay attention to the rapidly climbing

Mach numbers or the steady increasing heat of the cockpit windscreen.

Her concentration was focused entirely on her instrumentation arrays as she punched in coded sequences, flipped calibrated switches and turned dials to a variety of settings.

Actually, Gilroy's role on this run lay more in monitoring the situation than controlling it. An on-board diagnostic program was putting the system through its paces, testing every microchip, every high-definition camera lens, every component of the ulstrasensitive array of ELINT data probes.

It was stressing these critical elements to the limits of their performance envelope in order to make certain that the hardware and software were extracting every possible byte of data from the environment.

Cox leveled off the winged black needle at eighty thousand feet and threaded the SR through the microatmosphere which formed a thin blanket at the edge of space.

He knew that the SR had undergone physical changes during her recent "hot time."

Her fuselage had expanded, and the intense heat generated by the spyplane's multi-Mach flight speeds was making the fuel supply boil and bubble ever more rapidly within its storage compartments built into the hull, whose chine had even deformed in shape.

Now the aquamarine blue of the sky was all around him, stretching from horizon to horizon, attenuated like a thin plastic film drawn tightly around a large round fruit.

Yet overhead was the dark bowl of the black void lying beyond the fragile envelope of gases which surrounded the planet. The rest of the universe was just above him, and etched against it on Cox's forward horizon in intense blue was the faintly discernible curvature of the earth, which he and Gilroy had left behind only a short time ago.

One with the aircraft, Cox felt transformed and he thought of the Hindu gods worshipped by the Balinese, gods who sailed the skies on fiery chariots and whose exploits were celebrated in dance and song.

The Japanese too had likened the SR to creatures of myth. At Kadena in Okinawa, they had christened the sleek black plane *habu*, due to its resemblance to a local black serpent said to have magical powers, giving rise to the Habu patches which were awarded to SR pilots following their first operational mission.

A euphoric state overcame Cox, and memories of his friend Suteng, master of the sacred dances, resplendent in his ceremonial mask and robes as he reenacted the exploits of the warrior gods of the ancient myths, flooded into his mind.

"How are you holding up, Gilroy?" Cox asked the RSO after a check of the plane's instruments showed that its internal systems had settled into the hot-running mode of supersonic, high-altitude cruise.

"Doing just fine, boss," she told Cox.

"Great, kid," he replied, again remembering that this was Gilroy's first nonsimulator flight and recalling the butterflies in his own stomach on his first SR-71 check ride. "It's a little scary at first, but don't worry—it gets even scarier."

"Thanks for telling me," she replied sarcastically. "And by the way, congratulations."

"What for?" Cox asked.

"You just called me 'kid,' " Gilroy said. "Tells me there might be some kind of human being beneath that shitty exterior of yours."

Cox responded to this observation by saying, "Not a chance," and continued to put the Blackbird through her paces. Soon Cox saw that he was nearing the end of his journey.

He executed a wide, low-g turn and wheeled the supersonic aircraft around to begin the final leg of its mission, which would slingshot the plane back across Colorado and Nevada and bring it back to its covert hangar.

Back at the Black Hole, Martin Holloway and the SR's ground support crew were tracking the Blackbird on the support facility's wide-aperture radars. It was apparent that the SR-71 was performing well, performing like the trouper that the twenty-seven-year-old veteran was.

Holloway nodded his head as the R/O pointed out that the aircraft was operating at close to Mach 3.7, somewhat beyond its performance envelope, without a hitch.

Now it was time for the Blackbird to be cycled through its final test-flight routine. This was to be the test firing of its remote-targeted cruise missile.

"Motherbird to Raven," Holloway said into the handset of ground-to-air commo equipment. "Come in, Raven."

"This is Raven," Cox told the ground crew chief, "reading you five by five."

"You're looking good up there, Raven. I want you to get ready to deploy Highwire on the target aircraft," he informed Cox. "The drone should be coming your way any minute now. Have fun."

"Roger, Motherbird," Cox responded. "I plan to."

Soon Cox saw the target icon pop up on his radar scope, now set to a medium-range tracking mode. This was a superannuated F-4 Phantom that was being remote-piloted from the ground installation. The blip was closing with the SR from a distance of fifty miles.

Cox clicked on the icon on his tactical screen, which

selected the Highwire air-launched cruise missile from its main computer menu. The panels concealing the compartment in the belly of the Blackbird which housed the missile retracted, and the ALCM's launch dispenser was lowered below the fuselage.

Acquiring the target drone on the aircraft's newly installed AN/APG-67 radar set for air-combat acquisition, Cox deployed the ALCM on IR-seeking mode. The SR yawed to port as he felt it go, and he watched the missile streak ahead of the cockpit on launch, then abruptly veer aside as its seeker head locked onto the heat-emitting engine nacelles of the target aircraft.

Although the drone jinked and began a series of evasive sideslips, rolls and dives, the Highwire closed with the target in minutes.

A bright flash lit up the sky a moment later as the Highwire round detonated in a devastating airburst, followed by a dull, distant boom.

There was nothing left of the target aircraft following the explosion except for shards of flaming wreckage falling to earth. The drone aircraft had been utterly destroyed.

Ground-based high-speed tracking cameras had captured the sequence of events, however, and the footage would be studied by DARPA analysts at The Arcade prior to the finalizing of the mission in order to fine-tune the ALCM's performance parameters for maximum effectiveness.

From Holloway's vantage point, standing in the mission command center, though, the ALCM's performance merited a standing ovation.

"That wraps it up, Raven," he said to Cox via ground-to-air commo. "Bring the bird back to nest. Over to you."

"Roger, Motherbird," said Cox into his helmet mike and put the SR into a controlled decel/descent.

On the base firing range, Cox watched the demonstration of the weapon that was being issued to Gilroy and him as personal-defense side arms.

The range instructor had given both SR pilots a rundown on the capabilities of the firearm, which was an entirely new hybrid, a cross between a bullpup assault rifle and a submachine gun.

"This is the Fabrique Nationale P-90," he'd stated, showing them the advanced-design small arm, which did indeed look highly exotic to Cox. Seen head-on, it resembled something like a gray plastic doughnut. "For want of a better term, we'll call it a CAW, for close-assault weapon," the instructor went on in his preliminary remarks.

Everything about the weapon seemed revolutionary. It had been designed from the ground up around the newly developed 5.70 mm cartridge, the range instructor said. This was a smaller round than the conventional 9 mm ammunition fired by SMGs, but one which transferred far more of its energy on terminal ballistics.

The end result of this hybridization was unmatched stopping and piercing power minus the recoil and muzzle climb generally associated with all other comparable small arms.

In addition to these revolutionary features, the P-90 was also completely ambidextrous. Its shell casings were softly ejected by a "drop-down" process through a breech at the bottom of the receiver housing.

"Get a feel for the weapon," the instructor said to his pupils, handing each one a firearm. Both Cox and Gilroy hefted their CAWs.

Weighing under twelve pounds, the weapons were incredibly light in weight, and Cox felt embarrassingly as though he was holding a toy, and that this was all some sort of practical joke. The weapon not only felt ridiculously light, it also looked ridiculously ineffective.

"It's light," the instructor commented. "Hardly feels like it'll do anything. But you're wrong if you think that. Watch."

The instructor pulled his P-90 from a special Velcro speed-draw rig worn across his chest and pumped off a lightning burst of 5.70 mm ammo at a motorized paper target.

The ensuing three-round salvo was quick and the gun hardly moved at all. There was little sound too as the rounds were fired. Yet the burst had produced results: the paper target was patterned with an assortment of holes perfectly placed in the zones identified as vital strike points.

"Now you two try it," the instructor said, making certain that they held the CAW with its scissor-type buttstock pressed up against the crooks of their arms to further stabilize the highly controllable weapon.

Cox squeezed off a burst, discovering to his disbelief that he hardly felt the rounds being discharged.

His experience with firearms was limited to the Browning .45 caliber High-Standard semiautomatic pistol and the M16A1 assault rifle. Neither of the two performed anything like this little weapon, which outclassed them by miles.

The range instructor watched both Cox and Gilroy with a critical eye. The woman was doing okay for herself, he thought. She was punching paper with the best of them. In fact, she was doing somewhat better than Cox himself, although the range instructor would be the last person to tell that to Cox, especially while he was holding a loaded weapon in his hand.

Moscow

For the second time in as many weeks, the President of the Russian Republic huddled with the KGB chief in the bugproof room in order to be briefed on the progress of the covert mission which Valery Samsonov had been tasked with organizing.

The President's mood was as dark as the snow-cloud-laden skies which now brooded above Moscow.

Only last night, there had been another border incident in the Ukraine involving several deaths as armed paramilitary commandos struck Customs outposts established by the breakaway republic in a bloody surprise attack. In the Crimea too, there was new unrest as resurgent Communists sought to capitalize on that republic's inability to form a stable government or tame runaway inflation.

"Tallin's team is ready," Samsonov reported to the Russian President, delivering the first piece of reasonably good news that Pavlovich had heard in days. "He is a bitter man, but I believe he was the right choice. The vasaltnicki team he has put together appears to be in a full state of readiness. I personally witnessed field exercises in Zagorsk just this morning. I can report full confidence in their abilities for carrying out the mission."

"So all that is now lacking is my order to proceed," the President said after a brief pause. "The General Secretary's official blessing."

"Precisely," Samsonov responded immediately.

The Russian leader sat down at his desk and faced Samsonov. He regarded his old comrade for several long minutes.

In the nature of the homeland's current troubles lay the supreme irony, he mused: the Russian Republic's chief priority had historically been defense against invasion, a national obsession which had been shaped by successive waves of attackers from the ancient Tartars to Hitler's Wehrmacht.

This had been the rationale behind the establishment of the buffer at East Bloc client states during the Cold War years and explained why the Baltic provinces had been denied autonomy with such intransigence up until the time that the Kremlin had become powerless to prevent it.

The preoccupation with safeguarding the Russian heartland at all costs had colored every nuance of political thinking and had helped fuel the distrust with which the Soviets had looked upon the rest of the world.

Yet now, perhaps for the first time in the Rodina's history, grave threats to Russia were emerging not from the armies of foreign despots but from within her own borders. A further irony was the fact that the iron hand of secrecy which the Party had formerly wielded with impunity even after its demise, and which could always be counted on to mask unpleasant realities, was now more a hindrance than a help.

The operation now being contemplated would be completely back-channel in nature. The new realities of global politics made it imperative that the threat be dealt with quickly and, above all, quietly.

Pavlovich had been brooding for weeks about what would happen to his regime if it was perceived by the world that the crumbling Commonwealth had sunk to such abysmal new depths.

The repercussions would be unendurable, and they would come not merely from the Americans. The Germans, the French and the British—the staunchest advocates of loan guarantees to Russia—also would all stiffen their resistance, rescind promises of aid until they had satisfied themselves that the Commonwealth was not in imminent danger of civil war.

"Go ahead, Samsonov," the President advised his friend. "Tell Tallin that I sanction the mission. Let him go and do it quickly. And impress upon him that the fate of Russia may depend on how well he carries it off."

"I have already informed him of this," Samsonov told the President with the ghost of a smile playing across his lips. "And you need not worry. Tallin will not fail to carry out his mission."

Eastern Russian Republic, C.I.S.

The general awoke early. Again his sleep had been troubled by phantoms which had haunted his dreams. Yet these were not the vengeful ghosts of the Afghan dead.

In this present case, Aleksiev knew that these specters were real in a distinct sense: they were the mind's shadows of forces which his intelligence network had indicated were already mobilizing against him.

A window of opportunity was now open, but it might soon be closed. In order to win the high-stakes game, Aleksiev was aware that he would have to strike a devastating blow with lightning speed. Yet he could not do so, not precisely yet, at any rate.

Weapons of awesome destruction were in place and

his troops were dedicated and psychologically motivated to carry out the mission. Momentum was carrying all of them forward at breakneck speed, and, like him, his men believed it to be their sacred duty to ensure that the republic would not be destroyed.

Nevertheless, there were certain final arrangements yet to be carried out: the general was a meticulous soldier who was aware that to strike before all his assets were in place was to risk losing the fight.

Patience would see to it that he would succeed in his bid for supremacy. The general would not allow the ancient enemies of the Rodina, nor those weakhearted cretins in the Center, to destroy the homeland.

In visions he foresaw the nuclear holocaust which would befall both superpowers. Millions would die; this would be unavoidable.

However, the war would be quickly over: the nature of his offensive strike and the Americans' own strategy of countersurveillance would ensure that engagement would be broken off before the escalation ladder was climbed to its highest rung of mutually assured destruction.

From the smashed wreckage of the old regime, he would rise to lead those faithful to the Marxist-Leninist workers' Utopia who had pledged their lives to preserve the glorious dream of Communism from those who wished to wipe it utterly from the face of the earth.

This was to be the final outcome, and its time was growing nearer with each passing moment. He would exercise patience and orchestrate things properly; he would trigger a domino chain of events which would gather momentum of its own.

The general consulted his wrist chronometer. He had already created his chain of dominoes. It was now time to flick over the first domino in the chain and set events in inexorable motion.

The Black Beret troops were already in position outside the town of Novi Strelka in the Russian Republic. Like the outer republics before it, the district of which the town was the capital had been making ominous breakaway noises for some time, even going so far as to set up Customs checkpoints as the Ukrainians had first done two years before.

The commanders of the Black Beret units drawn from special forces troops were loyal to the Center, though, and even more loyal to the general himself.

On Aleksiev's command, the clandestine commando forces would sweep in like an avenging blood tide and embark on a campaign of mass slaughter. Unlike the case in past attacks, they would now be wearing the uniforms of regular Russian infantry troops and would massacre civilians with impunity.

After that, the outpost commanders would call in columns of troops and mechanized armor. These drastic measures would all be justified in the name of the restoration of order.

The world would accept this rationale. After all, much the same had taken place in Kiev a year or so before. Yet in this present case, the assault would be nothing more than a diversionary tactic engineered to deliberately conceal the general's actual purpose, one which would have far-reaching consequences for centuries to come.

Aleksiev picked up the phone on his desk and punched in a speed-dial number, setting events in motion which would change the direction of human history forever, and usher mankind into the time of the true workers' paradise.

12

Novi Strelka, Russian Republic

At 0420 hours, the recently established Customs checkpoint at the border of the breakaway district was deserted and tranquil. Guards in O.D. fatigues porting AKMs patrolled the lighted booths, some smoking cigarettes while others listened to music from a local station playing tinnily over a portable radio.

Ever since the breakaway district had declared its independence from the rest of the Russian Republic and had established the Customs checkpoint on its eastern border as a tangible symbol of this unilateral autonomy, there had been tensions resulting in outright hostility.

The Russian military bases and paramilitary police forces were not staffed with local personnel. They shared no sentiment for autonomy and remained loyal to the Center.

Skirmishes had erupted in the months since the checkpoint had been set up and there had been some injuries sustained on both sides. Tonight the guards were cautious, though not overly so.

The campaign of organized harassment had diminished lately in the wake of the recent Summit meeting between the U.S. President and the C.I.S.'s President, and there was even talk in the wind of political overtures which might ultimately lead to something more real in the way of autonomy than some hastily thrown up checkpoints on a desolate mountain frontier.

From out of the night, the commando death squads appeared.

The attackers wore black berets and woodland camouflage fatigues, though the uniforms bore no insignia whatever. Their faces cammied in nonreflective black, the commandos deployed around the checkpoint and immediately opened up with massed assault weapons fire.

The checkpoint guards returned fire but were quickly taken out. The assault force of Black Berets lobbed incendiary grenades into the checkpoint. The structure exploded into a bright ball of fire which soared hundreds of feet into the black, brooding winter sky.

In the orange glow given off by the flame-engulfed buildings, armored vehicles roared into the town. Paramilitary men, wearing the feared black berets and positioned behind the RPK machine guns mounted atop the BMPs, stood guard while troops deployed through the town square.

Lights were coming on in buildings surrounding the square as the invaders began kicking in doors. The bolt clatter of automatic firearms increased in tempo, as did the screams of the dying. . . .

Washington, D.C.

". . . late-breaking details of the violent crisis which has broken out early this morning in the town of Novi Strelka in the eastern Russian Republic. Reports are conflicting at this time, however . . ."

The President picked up the remote unit and zapped CNN to switch over to one of the network stations.

Humphries Van Zandt was on ABC, reporting another aspect of the same story.

". . . commandos wearing fatigues without insignia and black berets apparently stormed the Customs checkpoint at Novi Strelka in an early morning raid which left at least eight people dead and sixteen wounded. There are conflicting reports that the city has now been placed under martial law . . ."

The President zapped again, this time switching to CBS, where Arthur Mayhew sat behind the anchorman's desk and reported on the same story.

". . . as yet, no Western camera crews have been allowed in. It's hard to get a clear sense of what is taking place in Novi Strelka because all we can go on at this point are scattered eyewitness accounts. However, our sources paint a picture of complete discord and tell us there is fierce fighting taking place at this moment. For an analysis of these events, let's go to our Pentagon correspondent, Harry—"

Damping the gain on the audio, the President allowed the Pentagon correspondent to speak soundlessly on the hundred-inch flat-screen television and turned to Secretary of State Ben Franklin Cash, who sat behind him.

At the moment, they were thirty thousand feet off the plains of northern Iowa, en route to address a conference on farm subsidies via Air Force One.

"What has State's Consular Operations been able to add to this?" he asked Cash, who glanced at the soundless screen and leaned forward on his leather-backed chair.

"Not much, I'm afraid," he replied with a shrug. "With our satellite capability severely compromised, Cons Ops has been forced to rely on HUMINT sources, just like the networks. What they tell us is pretty much the same as the networks. The consensus with our colleagues from Langley and Meade seems to be that what's going on is a play by a heretofore unknown GRU hard-liner group to establish a power base in the Russian Republic."

"That doesn't make sense," the President answered with a frown. "Pavlovich has his strongest constituency there. He knows that our latest aid package—the biggest yet, I might add—is strongly tied to a cessation of precisely the kind of human rights violations that stopped the last one cold in Congress a few months back. He would be smart enough to keep his ear to the ground."

"Pavlovich might be pandering to the hard-liners in the military," Cash replied. "His power base is firmly entrenched there. Without it, he's nothing. He's compromised before and denied culpability in order to stay in power. It may be that the same situation now prevails."

"Yes, I suppose that could explain it," the President returned. "But I don't know if I can buy what the Central Intelligence spin doctors are putting out. The Russians have been able to live with the breakaways for a long time now. Sure, there have been border skirmishes, but nothing on the order of this—" He gestured at the Umbra-coded CIA analysis that he had just received via secure tactical digital facsimile, and which indicated that the extent of the military presence in the region was far greater than anything the news media had been able to piece together so far. "We're talking massive, brutal repressive measures, people being summarily imprisoned. You know what this reminds me of?" he asked Cash.

The Secretary of State nodded, having perceived the obvious parallel to which Bancroft was alluding. "Sure, it's the Iraqi invasion of Kuwait revisited. And there are even a couple of oil fields in the region."

"Yes, but there's more to it than even that," the President said. "There's also a wild card in the deck that, with the Kuwaitis or, for that matter, the Iraqis, was never in the picture: nuclear missile bases. And we're talking heavy stuff here, SS-18 long-range ICBM missile silos, with enough throw weight to knock us back to the Stone Age."

With his own words, the President had finally made up his mind to act. The need to take decisive steps, he realized, could be postponed no longer.

Webster Bancroft picked up the handset on the phone console in front of him and again direct-dialed the Kremlin. Bancroft would speak to the Russian President one final time, although he was certain that the crisis situation was already too far gone by this point for his conversation to have any real impact at all.

The repeated tones linking him to a phone six thousand miles away might signal the death knell of the human race.

13

Svalbard, Norway

The desolate island lay thirty degrees above the Arctic Circle. It was a barren expanse of wave-tossed rock inhabited by colonies of seals and dotted with the few isolated homesteads of its human natives. It was also a longtime takeoff point for covert reconnaissance flights into Commonwealth airspace.

On a clandestine runway sat the SR-71, which had been flown there by a two-man CIA crew to await the arrival by C-130 transport of the Watchtower flight personnel. Near the SR-71 were a series of thirty-five-foot-long, weather-resistant Amfuel bladders.

The bladders held a combined volume of nearly five hundred thousand pounds of JP-7 aviation fuel mixed with the dedicated high-temperature sealant which would maintain the stability of the fuel supply throughout the tremendous stresses of the SR's flight envelope. A pump was filling the Blackbird with the fuel mix while a ground crew went over its engines and other on-board systems in the subarctic cold.

While the SR-71 was taking on fuel in preparation for the mission, a CIA frigate was standing to offshore. The hold of the Glover-class frigate was crammed full of electronic gear, its radars and lasers continuously monitoring the electronic environment of the operations zone. On its aft deck a Blackhawk helicopter stood ready for immediate takeoff.

The frigate would serve as the forward analysis station for surveillance products brought back by the SR-71, as well as a seaborne support facility for search-and-rescue operations and heliborne retrieval of paradropped intelligence data.

The Blackhawk rotorcraft would deploy a SEAL amphibious unit toward an ocean drop zone for podded data records jettisoned by the SR, recovering these for analysis by the frigate's intelligence crew.

Elsewhere on the island, a KC-135Q Stratotanker aircraft specially outfitted as a dedicated air-to-air refueling (AAR) platform for the SR spyplane was parked beneath camouflage tarp.

As currently configured, the SR-71 could undertake missions of up to fourteen-hour durations.

The secret of flying these prolonged missions lay in the plane's ability to RV with the tanker in order to take on additional fuel reserves.

When the SR-71 had completed the first leg of its aerial reconnaissance mission, the KC-135Q Stratotanker aircraft would take off from the runway on Svalbard.

Flying under the curtain to avoid Russian forward-staring HEN HOUSE radar arrays looking toward the Pacific, the KC-135Q would fly to its assigned loiter zone.

There the SR-71 would rendezvous with the aircraft and refuel in midair. The tanker crew of the KC-135Q was specially trained in gassing up the SR planes and would carry out the refueling mission without a hitch.

With all the ducks in line, Dan Cox watched Gilroy ascend the metal steps of the wheeled boarding platform which stood to one side of the SR-71's cockpit, the plane's twin black cockpit hatches canted backward

in their unsecured positions. Gilroy swung herself into
the RSO's seat aft of the cockpit with practiced ease,
despite the bulky flight suits which both she and Cox
wore.

Cox followed his backseater up the stairs after she
had harnessed herself into the seat, and climbed into the
pilot's cockpit up top. One of the ground crew technicians helped dog down the cockpit hatches and flashed
Cox the thumb's-up sign. Cox responded with the same
gesture as he began to run through his preflight
warm-up routine.

His number one engine started up flawlessly, as did
engine two a few moments afterward. The chiclets on
his flight control panel were now all reading green.
Members of the ground crew had already swung aside
the boarding platform, while others were removing the
wheel chocks from the Blackbird's front and rear landing gear.

Cox now watched the ground controller holding up
the green lightsticks as, with expert motions of his
hands, he gestured to indicate that all was clear for the
Blackbird to begin to taxi toward the runway.

Cox eased the black ship's throttle forward and immediately felt the powerful Pratt & Whitney engines
whine in response as the SR pivoted on its massive
landing gear and pointed its sleek black nose assembly
toward the runway, which stretched into the distant horizon.

Within minutes, the Blackbird was taxiing down the
runway, its red hazard lights flashing.

Cox performed a final systems check as the CIA
crew chief on the ground consulted his instruments and
gave Cox clearance for immediate takeoff.

Having received final clearance, Cox pushed the
throttle forward and grasped the aircraft's control stick
in his other hand.

The SR-71 immediately responded, sprinting forward along the runway at an increasing rate of speed as Cox continued to ease the throttle forward and pull back on the stick until, with a sudden lurch, the spy craft's landing gear left the ground and the thunderous roar of the plane's engines filled the air.

With her nose pointing at the light-streaked postdawn sky, the Blackbird began to swiftly climb on a tail of fire as she gained altitude with great speed, announcing her departure with the SR's signature double sonic boom.

Minutes after leaving the airstrip, Cox reached his cruising altitude of seventy-five thousand feet.

Through the inch-thick heat-resistant glass of his cockpit windscreen, Cox enjoyed excellent conditions of visibility. Ahead, the blue sky was clear as crystal, its perfect blueness marred only by isolated wisps of high-altitude cloud formations.

Low over the eastern horizon, the sun glanced off the cockpit, throwing a multicolored kaleidoscopic effect across the control panels as Cox angled the Blackbird toward the southeast and switched over to autopilot navigational mode.

The sophisticated fly-by-wire system that had been retrofitted to the spyplane meant that the navigational computer had all the course coordinates programmed into its EPROM memory. Cox could override these at any time and he would constantly monitor the equipment in the event there was any need to make course changes.

Soon the Blackbird's southeasterly course heading brought the SR-71 across the Barents Sea and over Russian airspace, a fact which was echoed on the moving radar map display on the screen to Cox's right. The Blackbird's present position was indicated by a flashing arrow superimposed over a glowing electronic map of the Eurasian landmass racing past below them at the speed of a bullet exiting the muzzle of a gun.

Soaring high above the northern tier of the former U.S.S.R., the SR's preprogrammed mission profile immediately placed the on-board ELINT equipment into active mode.

The main console screen to Cox's top right flashed him the message that the electronic and photoreconnaissance camera pods mounted by the NSA techs in the five primary wells at port and starboard on the belly of the Blackbird were now subjecting the landscape below to a sophisticated multiple-mode scan.

In the seat behind Cox, Gilroy had already become absorbed in her tasks. In many respects, the RSO's duties on the mission were more important than those of the SR's pilot. As her computer display screens and liquid crystal readouts came alive, pouring out a steady data stream, she kept a constant watch on the intelligence which was being recorded in multimedia format.

It would be the backseater's prerogative to indicate if some special feature discovered below called for further investigation and a sudden departure from the original flight plan. Gilroy's blue eyes were alert, her fingers constantly busy at keypads and buttons, as the sky-challenging black needle plane cruised at the near edge of space.

Both Gilroy and Cox broke out tubes of soft food which they ate while working, inserting each tube through special holes located at the sides of their pressurized helmets and squeezing the nutrient paste into their mouths.

Munching a concoction labeled "chicken a la king," Cox thought to himself that, despite the revolutionary avionics and other advance retrofittings made to the SR, nobody had bothered to do anything about the chow: as far as he could tell, it had not changed a single bit since 1964. It was bad then and just as bad now.

Before long, Cox noted that their fuel supply was low enough to warrant returning to base. He notified Gilroy that they were heading back to the KC-135Q tanker's loitering area and punched in the course heading that would take the SR toward those coordinates along the aircraft's preplanned avenue of retreat, its "black line" back to safety.

As the Blackbird swung around to the northwest, neither member of its crew suspected that a Russian TU-126 MOSS platform had picked up their fleeting radar signature.

Inside the darkened cabin of the AWACS plane, the radar officer who had identified the contact had informed the crew chief of this sighting via internal commo.

Seated in his command center aft of the flight deck, the crew chief punched up the data on the wide-aperture radar screen in front of him, electronically looking over the R/O's shoulder at the screen, which had already lost the fast-moving blip.

"What do you think that was, sir?" the scope man asked the crew chief via the early-warning plane's intercom. The contact had been moving at Mach 3.6 and flying at far higher altitudes than any conventional aircraft would normally be expected to traverse.

Noting that a Sukhoi-27 Flanker aircraft was flying a combat air patrol circuit to the southeast, the crew chief ordered that the interceptor be sent in to investigate.

The Flanker's pilot received the search coordinates and, putting the Sukhoi on afterburner, screamed across the sky toward the place where the fleeting sighting had occurred.

Captain Yuri Magadan saw nothing, however, and radioed this fact to the MOSS aircraft, whose own long-range radars had by now lost the contact signature as well. Magadan was instructed in return to resume his normal patrol activities and to log a report.

The TU-126's crew chief, however, was a suspicious man. Barring instrument error, which did not appear to be the case, Commander Lev Borovich suspected that something quite real had triggered the radar sighting.

Borovich would make a note to be especially vigilant in the future: the general's mutiny had made all of those who followed him outlaws in their own land. Those who did not remain alert and suspicious in such times were doomed never to survive to enjoy the fruits of their treason.

14

Cox now had established visual contact with the KC-135Q Stratotanker call sign designated "Big Dipper" as the Blackbird approached the large aircraft's loiter zone.

The air-to-air refueling aircraft was flying a holding pattern in a tight circle at an altitude of twenty-six thousand feet above the waters of the Arctic Ocean, as close to Commonwealth airspace as it could safely venture without announcing its presence to Russian phased-array DOG HOUSE radars in a manner that would light them up like a Christmas tree.

In the cockpit of the Stratotanker, computerized AN/APG-65 radar was already locked onto the SR-71 photoreconnaissance aircraft and tracking it as the spyplane synchronized speed with the much larger jet aircraft. The KC-135Q's AN/APG-65 radar had been tracking the Blackbird's progress for the past few hundred miles.

As soon as radar contact had been established, the KC-135Q's well-trained flight crew went into action, the Stratotanker's boom operator readying himself to "fly the boom" for the in-flight refueling mission.

The more than two hundred thousand pounds of aviation fuel which had been pumped into the nine underfloor fuselage tanks of the giant AAR aircraft were now being prepared for off-loading as the tanker crew made ready to lower the refueling boom from its bay in the belly of the plane.

Now Cox had matched the speed of the Blackbird with the speed of the larger, heavier aircraft, which cruised several score feet above the SR-71, its bulky fuselage blocking out the last few rays of the setting sun as the two planes flew west on parallel courses.

"Ready to lower away at you," the flight engineer of the KC-135Q said in Cox's ear. "Open her up for me."

"Glad to oblige," Cox replied through the commo and flipped the toggle switch on the panel to his right. This raised the SR's hydraulically actuated fuel cowl into an upward position, exposing the longitudinal groove that ran along the spine of the fuselage aft of the rear cockpit and which would permit the winged nozzle of the fuel boom to align itself perfectly with the plane's fuel receptacle inlet.

Up above the SR-71, the boom crew flight engineer issued instructions to his tanker personnel to both lower and position the refueling boom until its nozzle interlocked precisely into place with the Blackbird's fuel receptacle inlet.

"Way to go!" one of the KC's crewmen shouted as the maneuver was executed.

"All right, open up the chocks," the flight engineer said into the bud mike of his head rig. "Let's get the bird all fueled up so we can get back to base."

"I'm for that, chief," said the boom operator as he deftly manipulated his two sidestick controllers, which actuated the computer-calibrated fuel pump, releasing the green flood of high-grade aviation fuel into the large rubber hose at a transfer rate of forty-five hundred liquid tons per minute.

The LCD readout on the instrument panel showed that the fuel in the KC's fuselage tanks was now flowing in a steady stream from the KC-135Q to the Blackbird below, and Cox could see his fuel-gauge readout numbers steadily climb as the SR thirstily drank in the JP-7.

Up in the tanker's central cockpit canopy, the flight engineer didn't bother with his instruments: when an SR was being refueled, the naked eye was just as good an indicator as the best available hardware.

Since the spyplanes carried fuel not only in most of the fuselage but in their "wet wings" as well, the surest indication that the Blackbird was full of avgas was when a cloud of JP-7 could be seen to spray from the seams of the aircraft's skin.

"That's it," the flight engineer shouted at his crewmen as he saw the telltale seepage begin. "We're out of here!"

The KC-135Q pulled the refueling boom back into her belly and the AAR plane's captain throttled down to fall behind the SR, then veered off on a course heading which would take the plane across the short stretch of the Barents Sea and back to the base on Svalbard Island.

The electronic data which had been paradropped to the ocean from the Blackbird in a special flotation pod sending out a transponder signal had already been retrieved by a SEAL unit standing down for this precise purpose, and was on its way to the CIA frigate anchored off the island's shoreline in the frigid sea via the Blackhawk UH-60 chopper.

Within an hour, the preliminary mission data gathered on the SR's intelligence run would be pored over by a team of NSA and CIA analysts making up the special task force of Operation Watchtower.

Punching a new command set into the plane's NAV computer, Cox nosed the Blackbird skyward for the second and final leg of its two-tiered mission. The first seven hours of flight had brought him and Gilroy across the southeastern search corridor of the northern Russian Republic. The second seven-hour leg of the grueling fourteen-hour surveillance mission called for a similar run to be made over Commonwealth airspace on an east–west axis.

The sky had darkened steadily and night had overtaken the northern hemisphere by the time the mission was moving into its first few hours of elapsed flight time.

As Cox cruised on a high-altitude flight trajectory which took the Blackbird on a soaring ride near the roof of the world, the enveloping blackness was all that he could see, broken only by the glow of the aircraft's computer VDTs and lighted instrumentation chiclets.

Many hours later, as the sun was just rising on the eastern horizon, Cox and Gilroy were looking forward to returning to Svalbard Island to conclude the mission.

Both surveillance pilots were feeling the effects of the many long, grueling hours of sitting in the SR's cramped cockpit as they cruised at supersonic speeds, and their bodies were fatigued by the severe stress of the mission as well as by the CIA-issue dexies they'd popped to remain alert.

Against the streaks of a magenta-colored dawn, the black *habu* snake screamed homeward on its long tail of fire.

Several hundred miles from the Blackbird, the Russian TU-126 electronic surveillance plane's FLAT JACK radars again picked up the mysterious blip that earlier had been tracked fleetingly. This time the R/O on board the aircraft had been ready to identify the contact signature and to instantly send up a fighter to visually identify the target.

The blip was moving every bit as quickly as the radar echo that had been detected the previous afternoon, and this time there could be no question whether or not this sighting was due to mechanical failure.

The signature was definitely that of an aircraft, and one that was flying amazingly high and proceeding at extremely great Mach numbers.

Dispatched by the MOSS, Captain Magadan in the SU-27 picked up the bogey on his own search radar minutes later. It was moving fast, and flying high, as he had been informed by the TU-126. The Russian fighter pilot had never seen anything move quite like it.

What sort of aircraft was he dealing with? he wondered. Surely it was not the American F117A, because even the Stealth fighter was not as fast or as maneuverable as the bandit on his pulse doppler search radar was behaving.

Whatever the bandit was, though, Magadan was confident that he would soon overtake it and discover the answer. Once he had identified the target, his orders were to report back to the AWACs craft and await further instructions. However, if the unknown aircraft was moving too quickly, he was to use his own initiative. To Magadan, this meant that he had the authority to shoot it down if necessary.

As Magadan was changing course, Cox also suddenly received warning as the long-range "fingerprinting" radars which the Blackbird had been retrofitted with flashed him the threat icon of an aircraft closing with the SR on a high-velocity pursuit profile.

According to the RHAWS, or radar heading and warning system data, the hostile aircraft was moving at a speed in excess of Mach 2.5 and closing quickly with his own craft.

Cox realized he was in trouble. The aircraft's radar signature identified it as a Sukhoi series Fencer or Flanker, and if the Blackbird was caught by such a fast, maneuverable and heavily armed plane, it would be an easy target despite its great speed and on-board passive ECM systems.

From hard experience in bimonthly surveillance flights high over the skies of Afghanistan, Cox knew that the only chance he and Gilroy now had of making it out of Russian airspace was to outdistance the fighter before its standoff weapons systems could lock onto the Blackbird's target profile.

Once they were within range of the AA-class missiles with which the Russian fighter was outfitted, it would be difficult to outrun and impossible to escape.

There were only seconds left in which to react and Cox made timely use of every one of them.

As he shunted the SR out of autopilot mode, adrenaline sending a rush of energy surging through his fatigue-stressed nervous system, Cox experienced what was almost tantamount to a strange feeling of relief.

At last the monotony of playing second fiddle to a glorified piece of silicon had given way to immediate action. Whatever happened next, Cox could at least feel secure in the knowledge that his fate was finally back in his own hands and out of the NAV computer's control.

Speeding on a northwesterly course heading at high Mach numbers, Cox sent the Blackbird into a straight yo-yo, performing a shallow twenty-degree dive to trade off altitude for speed, then pulled back the throttle and roared skyward on full afterburner, his eyes on the constantly refreshed screen of the long-distance radar, fixed on the glowing icon which represented the pursuing Russian fighter.

From the information flashed on his radar scope, Cox knew that the fighter pilot was pouring on the speed as well, intent on catching up with him.

He would see about that.

Cox felt the entire Beta B-120 titanium-alloy airframe savagely vibrate as he pushed the SR's design envelope hard, thrusting the Blackbird ever higher, knowing that the lives of himself and Gilroy depended on the Blackbird traveling higher and farther and faster than the formidably armed attack plane closing in on them.

The Sukhois were top performers, but they were far clumsier than the SR, whose engines were designed to breathe the microatmosphere at ninety thousand feet.

As the SR continued to gain altitude, the lightening dawn sky began giving way to seamless black, and the shuddering of the plane increased as its hull was subjected to stresses verging on the limits of its design capabilities.

An hour past the midpoint of their second recon leg, with much of its fuel having been burned off, the Blackbird was several hundred pounds lighter than it had been when they'd taken off from Svalbard, and he was able to get fractionally more speed out of the SR's airframe.

Still, Cox knew that he needed even greater speed, and this meant lightening the craft still further. Even if it meant depleting their fuel reserves and blowing their chances of making it back to base, Cox had to take the risk of carrying out the strategy he had in mind. Although the long-range radar showed that they were outdistancing the Russian fighter, the Sukhoi was still on their tail.

Hitting a series of lighted rocker switches, Cox dumped as much of the craft's fuel via the fuel dump tube, situated at the apex of the SR's tail cone, as he felt he could get rid of without immediately compromising their chances of ever returning to base.

Lighter now by an additional several hundred pounds, the Blackbird seemed to bolt forward like a horse let loose from its reins, climbing higher into the dark black sky of near space, her airframe shuddering violently. Contrails of superheated gas, caused by the ionizing effect of her speeding hull against the ozone in these high atmospheric regions, created a glowing halo effect around the cockpit.

Three hundred miles away and ten thousand feet below the sky-challenging Blackbird, Captain Yuri Magadan cursed in frustration as he watched the bandit disappear from his long-range radar scope.

Fine-tuning the forward-looking search radar didn't help either, and the MOSS as well had lost all track of the blip.

Magadan was ordered to return to base by the TU-126, and as he swung the Flanker around on a northeast flight trajectory, he swore that he would meet up with that bandit again, and next time the outcome would be considerably different.

The threat icon had disappeared from the radar screen moments before the Blackbird would have reached the upward limits of her performance envelope. As matters now stood, Cox believed that he had broken all records set for a steep, high-altitude climb in an SR-71. However, there was no time for self-congratulations, since they were not out of the woods yet.

Cox nosed the spyplane back down and saw that his fuel reserves were now at dangerously low levels. He throttled back and reduced thrust to a bare minimum, his fingers keystroking in the coordinates for their landing zone.

According to the readout he received from the SR's NAV system, Cox knew that they might barely make it if they conserved fuel and flew the rest of the way home on a powered glide.

Hours later, the ground crew on Svalbard Island let out a spontaneous cheer as they finally saw the telltale twin tongues of the Blackbird's Pratt & Whitney turbo ramjet engine exhaust track light up the seaward sky when Cox brought the SR in for a long-delayed three-point landing.

PART TWO

Fly the Black Line

15

Eastern Russian Republic, C.I.S.

The entire zone of operations had now been placed under martial law. The civilian radio stations that the vasaltnicki team constantly monitored provided the commando strike force with breaking situation reports concerning the anarchy that had gripped the breakaway district.

In order to avoid the mounting possibility of confrontation with local militia, which would almost certainly shoot first and ask questions later, Tallin and his commando force had moved off the road they had been following on their line of deployment. They had shifted instead to a strategy of navigating the land in the heavily forested timber country that stretched into the mountainous regions above.

The strike team deployed in a diamond formation: two men positioned on the left and right flank of the main squad element at a distance of twenty meters, with Piotr scouting ahead and Gennady at the column's rear.

The forest terrain became more heavily wooded as the commando unit ascended higher into the northern mountain range.

Accurate land navigation was facilitated by means of the two compact, hand-held global positioning system (GPS) units carried by the team, the same type of device first utilized in nonsimulated combat situations by Desert Storm forces.

The compact GPS systems were among the prizes which Tallin had received from the KGB, and only he and Piotr were allowed to use the innovative technical equipment. GPS electronically performed land-navigation calculations that had been tedious and inaccurate throughout the history of warfare.

Uplinked to the phased array of Navstar geostationary satellites parked in low earth orbit, each hand-held GPS could flash the holder's position on its LCD readout window and provide real-time navigational data to any point chosen that would be accurate down to plus or minus five yards.

Tallin carried military maps of the operations zone, but these were for backup purposes only, in the event that this orbital system suffered the blinding which had thus far been confined only to the superpowers' photoreconnaissance satellites.

The covert strike unit's present destination was Gody Nimovka, a region in the foothills of the Verkhoyansk Mountains, in which analysis of existing, though dated, satellite data provided by a SPOT survey satellite had revealed evidence of recent high-level construction.

Digitized and converted into a three-dimensional map display on a DEC-5000 computer, the finished intelligence indicated that a new road had been carved out along a ridgeline which overlooked a high valley.

The valley was wide enough to provide the space necessary for a functional air base with a landing strip sufficiently long to permit takeoff and landing by the Blackjack long-range bombers believed to be situated at the clandestine base.

Although gathered some months before, the data offered the most recent satellite intelligence available and the best guess as to the location of the vasaltnicki strike team's target.

It was now a little past 1100 hours, and the vasaltnicki team was ascending through steeply upsloping terrain thick with Siberian timber pine.

So far, weather conditions were satisfactory enough to permit making efficient progress by the vasaltnicki strike unit. There had been a low ground fog at daylight, but this had been burned off by the sun soon after sunrise. The commando team had then rested and consumed rations and had by now been climbing for the better part of an hour.

Tallin was consulting his GPS for one of his hourly position updates when he saw the figure in woodland-pattern BDUs running forward from the rear of the column. Tallin held up his hand in a signal for the unit to halt as Gennady, who had been trailing the unit thirty meters behind the main element, came up to him, breathing stertorously.

"There's a militia patrol about a hundred fifty meters behind us," he informed Tallin, gathering his thoughts to precisely and quickly relate the pertinent facts to the strike team's leader as he had been trained to do in such situations.

"How many of them, Gennady?" Tallin asked the commando.

"Thirty men, armed with Kalashnikovs," Gennady responded. "For militia, they appear professional. The weapons seem of recent issue and all are uniformed in woodland camouflage fatigues."

"Do you believe they are trailing us?" Tallin asked again.

"I'm not certain," Gennady responded at once, having anticipated the strike leader's following question. "I can't rule out that they may be, however."

Tallin considered for a moment while the unit gathered around him and Gennady.

Given the massive civil unrest which had broken out in this region during the days since the strike team's insertion, any and all contingencies had to be considered valid and responded to as serious threats.

Even if the unit was in fact being followed by the patrol trailing behind, it was unlikely that the militia had any inkling of who they were or what their mission was.

"We'll try to outdistance them," he told the team members, making his decision. "If we can't shake them, we'll hit them fast and hard."

To Piotr, who was acting as forward scout, Tallin also issued the order that he remain on the lookout for a good place to set up a kill trap in the event the unit was not able to shake the militia patrol.

"Let's move out," Tallin finally said.

Mobile again, the vasaltnickis doubled the speed of their march through the steep and treacherous woodland terrain.

After an hour of evasive maneuvers designed to throw off the militia patrol behind them, which included wading through streams and doubling back on their own tracks before breaking to one side, Tallin ordered the team to halt.

A few feet ahead, the trail paralleled a dry stream bed which, after another ten feet or so, widened into a hollow flanked by a granite ledge projecting about fifteen feet above the gully floor.

Piotr had cited this as an ideal place to set up an ambush point. Signaling to Gennady to move up to consult with him, Tallin confirmed with the rear-guard man that the patrol was still following them.

"They are still with us," Gennady again reported. "Their tracker is good."

Issuing rapid, concise orders for his men to take cover on the high ground above the hollow, and for the machine gunners to set up with the bipod-equipped Ultimax 100s they had requisitioned, Tallin quickly established the points at which he could best deploy butterfly mines in a phased array.

It would be a break of three, a tactic which Spetsnaz forces had perfected in dealing with the Afghanistani Mujahideen in the high mountain passes of the rugged hill country outside Kabul.

Unshipping three of the PFM-1 antipersonnel submunitions from his rucksack, Tallin positioned the first of the butterfly mines at the far end of the hollow, where it narrowed again. He inserted the directional antipersonnel submunition's pointed metal tripod deeply and securely into the soft earth so that the part of the butterfly mine which bore the cautionary message THIS SIDE TOWARD ENEMY was angled to discharge blast effect and preformed ten-millimeter ball shot down the length of the gully.

Repeating this same procedure with the remaining two butterfly antipersonnel devices, Tallin staggered them to the left and right of the hollow, spaced about six feet apart. The break of three would create a zigzag of blast effect which would trap the patrol in a lethal crossfire of thousands of metal balls, generating a high kill ratio.

From a secure position on the high ground overlooking the hollow, Tallin would detonate the first butterfly as soon as the patrol entered the kill trap. The resulting explosion would send the survivors running back toward the second butterfly charge, which would blast them again from a sixty-degree angle.

The survivors at the rear of the column would be taken out by the third butterfly, detonating a pulsebeat behind the first two charges.

A shock front of withering automatic fire from the Ultimax LMGs and Spectre submachine guns, in addition to APERS grenade airbursts, would ensure that none of the militia-patrol members survived the onslaught.

Minutes after deploying the butterflies, Tallin scrambled up to the heights above the gully. Crouching beside Piotr, he surveyed his handiwork, assuring himself that he had placed the antipersonnel submunitions for maximum lethality while checking the battery and signal strength indicator lights on the remote detonation device he held in his hand.

"Here they come," Piotr whispered moments later, staring in the direction of the approaching militia column.

Tallin saw the point man of the patrol unit suddenly appear on the far edge of the trail. He was moving cautiously, scanning the trail ahead of him for the vasaltnickis' spoor.

Tallin permitted himself to smile grimly as the patrol filed into the hollow behind the point man.

The commando's pulse quickened and his nostrils flared as the final two men entered the kill trap, and he held up his hand as a signal to his own troops, who silently deployed their weapons. A moment later, Tallin dropped his hand and simultaneously triggered the first butterfly charge.

A loud, sharp *crump!* came from a spot where a cloud of gray-brown earth and shattered rock was lifted high into the air as hundreds of steel balls shot toward the center of the patrol.

At the same time, the vasaltnickis were hurling massed automatic fire and APERS grenades into the center of the gully. As the main body of the patrol turned to run backward, Tallin triggered the second butterfly, and then the third, catching the survivors in an obliterating crossfire.

Less than a minute after Tallin had detonated the final butterfly charge, he held up his hand again and signaled for his men to cease firing.

Stillness now took hold of the forest again as, through a haze of acrid cordite smoke, the vasaltnickis looked down into the mass grave.

Hopelessly trapped inside the hollow, the patrol's members had been ripped asunder, and body parts as well as organ matter had been strewn all over the sides of the gully.

Ordering the main element of the squad to remain in position, Tallin took Piotr and Gennady down into the kill trench.

There were no survivors.

The carnage was total and the casualty count complete. Flies were already beginning to buzz around the bloodied heap of dismembered and mutilated corpses, and the air was filled with the stench of high-explosive smoke and the noxious odors of blood and entrails.

Ordering Piotr and Gennady to search the remains of the blast-mutilated corpses, Tallin signaled the all-clear to the rest of the unit, which now came down from the heights to look over the kill trench.

Some of the commandos gagged at the sight of the mass kill, but most had become all too familiar with tactics such as these and their results from Spetsnaz operations inside Afghanistan, especially during the culminating years of the war when the tempo and shape of the battle had risen to its fiercest pitch.

Soon Piotr and Gennady brought Tallin bloodstained sector maps and ammunition retrieved from amid the entanglement of enemy dead. Tallin ordered them to disburse the ammunition to the rest of the unit and studied the sector maps.

The intelligence which had been gathered by this means was highly interesting.

Spread out across a granite boulder, one of the captured sector maps displayed a red circle drawn around an area of mountain country lying about two hundred miles to the north. This particular area exactly paralleled the vasaltnicki team's own destination.

Pocketing the sector map retrieved from the corpse of the patrol member, Tallin consulted his GPS unit and ordered the team to hide the evidence of the kill trench and then move out quickly. The patrol would soon be missed and a search detail organized and deployed to ascertain its whereabouts.

The encounter with the militiamen complicated matters for the vasaltnickis. Tallin knew he would have to increase the pace of the unit's march. They might have more company soon, and in that event, would need to be prepared for an engagement with a warier and better-prepared oppositional force.

16

Svalbard Island

Cox and Gilroy sat in the briefing room of the inflatable Quonset hut that was part of the modularized mission-support facility set up near the covert landing strip. Mission control officer Martin Holloway stood in front of them, chain-smoking Marlboros as he made notes on a wheelable chalkboard that stood behind him.

After over fourteen hours of "hot time," the SR-71 was now being overhauled in the base hangar by its CIA maintenance crew while its ELINT and photo-reconnaissance sensors were purged of data and refitted to their deployment wells and fuselage blister pods. The spyplane would be refueled after the maintenance crew was finished with her.

"We think we've turned up some possibles," Holloway said to Cox and Gilroy, who sat on folding chairs, Cox sucking a vanilla milkshake through a straw while Gilroy leaned back, arms crossed and legs jutting out at an angle, balanced by sneaker heels on the concrete floor.

Cox heard the steady hammering of cold Arctic sleet drum without letup against the windows of the hut. One of the numerous squalls that regularly lashed across the island from the northwest at this time of the year was

now dumping an icy rain down on the Svalbard
mission-support facility.

Cox thought momentarily about flying an SR out
under such conditions, something he had never personally attempted: his flights had always originated under
carefully planned takeoff conditions, often from tropical
or arid landscapes at forward observation bases like Tak
Le in Thailand or Kadena, Japan. If ordered to do so he
would decline: the SR had never been proved reliable
under such adverse takeoff conditions.

"The strongest of these possibilities appears to be a
base in the eastern Russian Republic," Holloway went
on, using a laser pointer to indicate an area on the composite blowup made from the preliminary data which
had just come back from the NSA-CIA command post
in the frigate anchored offshore.

"It's especially interesting in light of the fact that this
location matches satellite reconnaissance photos taken
some months ago showing a rudimentary installation
then under construction. The installation shown here is
far more articulated, and parts of it are apparently cam-
ouflaged."

Holloway continued to inform Cox and Gilroy of the
fact that hangars identified at the target site appeared to
be large enough to house Blackjack nuclear bombers.

In one especially revealing shot among the hundreds
of individual frames which had been brought back by
the SR, an ambiguous surface area projecting from one
of the hangars had looked, to analysts detached from
the CIA's National Photographic Interpretation Center,
tantalizingly like that of the tip of one of the bomber's
readily identifiable canted, mission-adaptable wings,
which could be manipulated to compensate for changes
in airflow and speed conditions.

Flatbed trucks nearby were large enough to carry the
AS-15 long-range cruise missiles that the Blackjack

payloaded in complements of eight, each of which was capable of accurately delivering a one-megaton warhead to targets located across distances approximately two thousand miles, while flying below the threshold of radar surveillance.

"What the intelligence analysts tell me is that they now require another, close-in look at this site," Holloway told the Blackbird pilots, already anticipating exactly the reaction he received. Gilroy said nothing, but Cox was pissed off at being sent back out again so soon.

"Why not just nuke the installation, Holloway?" he ventured with calculated flippancy. "You and your spooks have seen enough recon photos to get your rocks off for a while. Gilroy and me have beaten the odds already. Next time we'll get our asses shot up and you know it."

"Don't be ridiculous, Cox," Holloway replied vexedly. "We have to be certain of our facts. If we aren't we can't make an informed assessment. This is especially true in light of the current situation prevailing in the central region. The turmoil shows signs of spilling over into the rest of the Russian Republic. The entire country could be plunged into a state of anarchy at any time."

There was more news of the same kind.

In eastern Russia the pot was boiling over.

The NSA had just delivered a report strongly suggesting that certain local commanders in charge of missile installations were threatening to launch the missiles in their arsenals if Moscow did not immediately recognize the autonomy of other regions of the vast Russian heartland as it had done to the sub-breakaway republics before.

The strategic situation was destabilizing rapidly. With orbital intelligence platforms knocked out, and high-altitude surveillance capability almost nonexistent, it was imperative that the Blackbird fly another mission as soon as the aircraft was ready to take off.

Mission commander Lev Borovich sipped hot coffee in the mission manager's compartment of the TU-126 electronic warfare reconnaissance aircraft, located forward of the crew area, a small alcove near the galley and aft of the cockpit. Borovich had been giving the matter of the mysterious radar contact considerable thought for some time now.

From the Sukhoi pilot's report he had gathered not only that the aircraft which had popped up on the scope flew at extremely high velocities and was greatly maneuverable, but that its flight envelope could take it to extraordinarily high altitudes. These data were not in conformance with other features typified by current aircraft designs fielded by any of the world's nations.

The sighting was most perplexing.

It was, however, in complete keeping with the flight profile of certain of the covert spy aircraft flown by the Americans until very recently—specifically, the SR-71 high-altitude photoreconnaissance aircraft.

If it was in fact an SR-71 Blackbird that had outrun and outmaneuvered the Flanker, then it would tend to confirm the rumors which Borovich had heard regarding the covert response to the disabling of Russian and American surveillance satellites by what to the world's leaders must surely be an unknown force whose intentions both mystified and terrified.

Of one fact Borovich was completely certain, however. This was that the pilot of the mysterious aircraft was a man of exceptional skills. His escape-and-evasion maneuver had caught the veteran Sukhoi pilot completely by surprise.

Borovich personally knew Magadan and he was

aware that the fighter jockey had taken being out-flanked by the aircraft he was chasing as a personal affront.

Indeed, Magadan had demanded first crack at the aircraft should it be picked up again. Borovich had promised Magadan that he would have his chance if ever the aircraft was again sighted on the MOSS's radar scopes.

He had the feeling that it would.

Cox was airborne within an hour after Holloway's intelligence briefing in the Svalbard Island mission-support facility. His muscles still ached from the previous two mission legs he had flown, but Gilroy's younger, more supple body didn't respond like his aging bones, or at least she didn't let on that she was feeling as stiff as Cox was.

With the Arctic squall petering out, the Blackbird took off from the clandestine runway through a light drizzle posing no threat of icing up the aircraft's moveable control surfaces. Cloud cover was low and dense, but visibility was good enough, so that Cox met with no difficulty in navigation by direct visual means.

At the covert airstrip on Svalbard, the ground crew watched the sleek black reconnaissance aircraft cant vertically as long tongues of scorching yellow exhaust flame streamed from the Blackbird's nozzle vanes as the SR-71's angle of climb increased to an ever-steeper altitude. Finally the Blackbird ascended above cloud level and vanished from sight of the unaided eye, thundering out its departure with double sonic booms.

The Blackbird was visible to ground-based tracking equipment, however. The ground crew's long-range radars monitored the rapidly moving signature appearing on their scopes, and Holloway in the installation's command-and-control center was able to watch the SR's progress on a southeasterly course heading which would ultimately bring the aircraft back across the Barents Sea and send it hurtling across Commonwealth airspace.

Holloway knew that this second reconnaissance run was stretching the chances of the mission's success to the maximum limits of probability, just as Cox had insisted.

The Blackbird had been designed to fly its missions during an era of military technology two generations behind the current state of the art. The SRs had ruled the skies before AWACS platforms routinely patrolled for intruder aircraft.

One of the reasons that the SR-71 program had been discontinued had been the increasing vulnerability of the spyplanes to detection from the long-distance, over-the-horizon backscatter radars fielded by EC-3A-class advance warning and detection systems platforms and the SRs' subsequent vulnerability to interception by increasingly faster and more formidably armed generations of Russian fighter aircraft.

Nevertheless, the vital mission that Cox and Gilroy were engaged in was important enough to warrant placing their own personal safety at risk.

If they had not been informed in plain terms before accepting the mission, both members of the Watchtower crew were professionals who were tacitly aware that they were expendable, their personal fates subverted to the greater good and the higher morality which they served.

In the cockpit of the SR-71A, already several hundred miles from the ground station where Holloway now walked away from the radar console, Cox watched as his moving-radar map readout showed his position just over the stretch of open water lying between Svalbard Island and the northern coast of Russia.

His thoughts reflected those of Holloway's. The close call with the Sukhoi fighter plane was not the last of their troubles, he knew.

Russian AWACS aircraft had undoubtedly stepped up surveillance activities in the wake of the initial sighting.

Unarmed, except for the single optomechanically guided terminal munition which the SR carried in its specially adapted bomb bay, the SR-71 was not capable of responding to threat situations by any other means than evasion-and-escape maneuvers.

Like that of the horse, the Blackbird's defense against her enemies was to outrun them, rather than to fight them on their own terms. Once the plane had ventured within the lethal perimeter of a hostile aircraft's offensive systems, the SR-71 was one of the most vulnerable craft in the sky.

Cox would have to be ready for anything. And he would have to expect the worst. Because the worst was almost certainly bound to happen.

17

The black-hulled reconnaissance aircraft skimmed on a low-trajectory, radar-evading flight path over the wave-tossed surface of the Barents Sea, using the added lift of surface effect to conserve fuel. Once it neared Commonwealth territory, its mission profile computer returned control of the SR to Cox.

Opening up the throttle full out, Cox shunted the Blackbird into afterburner and climbed to the upward limits of the spyplane's performance envelope, to a cruising altitude of eighty-five thousand feet above the wrinkled ancient ranges of mountains which rose below on the C.I.S.'s northern boundary.

Already terrain-mapping radars and multiple ELINT recording sensors were activated by the SR-71's on-board control computer. Invisible low-energy laser beams produced by a microwave energy pump lanced down through the thin cloud cover, following every contour of the terrain below, mapping it into silicon memory.

Every feature of the landscape traversed by the probing track of the sensing laser was immediately digitized by terrain-mapping computers on board the Blackbird. These impressions were logged permanently on a single rewritable compact disk whose data load would be dumped into intelligence computers on the craft's return to its point of origin.

Gilroy again scanned her array of screens and instrumentation chiclets as Cox leveled the Blackbird out and shifted the aircraft back to navigational computer control, the changeover signaled by a two-note electronic beep tone from the tiny speaker grille set in the console panel.

Cox scanned his own instrumentation banks, noting that the SR-71 was reading green in all critical areas. Fuel consumption remained at acceptable levels, electrical systems were adequately powered and all other systems were functioning at high efficiency.

Yet Cox was on edge: he knew that invisible trip wires had been strung across the skies over Russia.

He knew that distant, unseen guardians of Russian airspace were keeping their vigil at the electronic watchtowers of long-range detection systems, and that weapons of awesome destructive power could be deployed at the touch of a button to bring the SR down in a nosedive toward flaming destruction.

At 0820 hours, chief flight officer Lev Borovich received a voice transmission from his chief R/O over the surveillance plane's intercom system.

It was a transmission which Borovich had been eagerly awaiting for several hours. The message stated that the mysterious aircraft had been sighted once again, this time while traversing Russian airspace in a southeasterly direction.

The American spyplane had been sent in for another reconnaissance mission, Borovich thought to himself. In the interim between the two sightings he had convinced himself that the aircraft had of necessity to be an SR-71 Blackbird, redeployed by the Americans or their NATO allies.

While the Europeans were continuously fielding TR-1s on intelligence-gathering runs, these craft did not

possess the greater speed, maneuverability or performance capabilities that the Blackbirds did. They were
superior to the SR only in their advanced electronic intelligence collection payloads.

No, there could be no question about it, Borovich
was sure. The Blackbird had been redeployed above the
skies of Russia.

Borovich's thoughts raced back to a time some fifteen years before, when, as the radio officer of a
MiG-29 fighter plane, he had experienced his first encounter with an American SR-71.

Borovich and the pilot were flying the plane over the
Black Sea. This was a flight corridor notorious for the
fact that it was used routinely—had been for over a decade—by American spyplanes taking off from covert
CIA bases in northern Turkey.

The MiG pilot's voice suddenly was heard in the
backseater's earphones, proclaiming that he'd sighted a
fast-moving blip on his radar scope flying at extremely
high altitudes and was pursuing the bogey.

Soon the MiG had made visual contact with the unknown airborne object, and Borovich now recalled that
he had marveled at his first sighting of the swiftly moving black aircraft, which could be seen knifing across
the skies a few miles ahead and high above them, a
small black speck at the apex of a spreading contrail of
white exhaust gases.

At first Borovich and the MiG pilot were both convinced that they had sighted a missile, believing that no
aircraft could move as quickly as this was going. Each
of them believed for a long, terrifying time-beat that
they were witnessing a nuclear first strike on their
homeland.

However, moments after the sighting, the SR-71 began to take evasive action, climbing rapidly as its AN/
ASG-18 radar picked up the MiG, and both pilots

breathed sighs of relief: only a piloted aircraft could behave in such a manner.

The MiG gave chase and had fired 23 mm cannon rounds at the Blackbird without managing to hit the fast-moving aircraft.

Climbing steadily higher as the SR gained altitude, the pilot of Borovich's fighter was about to fire one of his AA rockets when suddenly the MiG's engine failed and suffered total burnout at eighty thousand feet, its air-breathing engines unable to sustain combustion at the microatmosphere at that height.

The MiG went into a sudden stall as the pilot tried unsuccessfully to restart the fighter's engines, and Borovich remembered having watched the SR-71 speed skyward, the fiery trails of its afterburner exhaust seeming to mock the dire predicament of the two Russian fliers.

Borovich and the pilot both pulled between their legs the striped yellow levers which blew the explosive bolts beneath their ejector seats and catapulted them into the air.

Borovich's parachute opened as it was supposed to; however, the pilot's chute did not.

Borovich shuddered involuntarily as he recalled how he had witnessed the doomed pilot drop past him like a stone, a look of horror etched on his face, his rate of descent becoming faster and faster, until he had vanished entirely from view a heartbeat later.

Now Borovich would settle the score that he had owed the Americans for fifteen years.

He would bring down a Blackbird!

Now flying across the northeastern C.I.S. and passing directly over the wooded slopes of the mountainous region of the Russian Republic, a region on the frontier of Russia, the SR-71 was into the middle phase of its computerized ground-mapping routine.

While Cox monitored his scopes and chiclets in the cockpit of the spyplane, Gilroy—in her RSO's compartment behind the pilot's area—checked her own highly specialized gear and watched as the instruments showed the results of the multiple-mode scanning operations which they undertook.

The plane was now overflying the area of the mission's central focus. This was the region which had been identified as the principal site of the clandestine air base high in the Verkhoyansk Mountains.

Gilroy punched up a real-time display on one of her nondedicated VDTs and, using a series of keystroked command lines, continued to fine-tune the image and resolution of the enhanced video picture until she had a clear, bird's-eye view of the installation now below them.

Gilroy could accurately pick out detailed features of the target zone now. The real-time video data, amplified and cleaned up by digital imaging technology, showed with distinct clarity that a plane with the Blackjack's configuration was being housed in one of the hangars. There was activity throughout the general base area as well.

"Have a look at this, boss," Gilroy said as she pumped this data into Cox's CPU up front, using a trackball cursor to point out specific features more than eighty-five thousand feet below the high-flying plane.

"Jeez," Cox replied into his helmet mike, "there's a guy down there with his fly open." Both he and Gilroy shared a laugh.

Cox screened the real-time photoreconnaissance data and knew intuitively that they had hit paydirt with this run. But he was getting edgy as the final few minutes of data collection elapsed and all of the SR-71's sophisticated electronic scanning devices were turned on.

When the high-risk surveillance operation was concluded, Cox gratefully set a course heading which would point the Blackbird's blended chine nose in the direction of Norwegian airspace, following his line of retreat back to Svalbard Island, where the SR-71's data could be downloaded and where Cox could finally leave the stress of the mission behind him.

As it turned out, nothing would be further from the truth.

18

In the cockpit of the Sukhoi Flanker, Captain Yuri Magadan was awaiting the confirmation of the reported sighting.

Ten kilometers distant from the AWACS platform as he patrolled the skies above the northern C.I.S., Captain Magadan heard the voice of the TU-126's R/O suddenly crackle in his headphones.

The radio operator's voice was informing the Sukhoi pilot that the SR-71 had been conclusively sighted and apprised Magadan of its present position, speed and heading.

Before long, the Flanker's long-range radar display lit up as lobes of pulse doppler microwave energy bounced off the target aircraft and were reflected back into the Flanker's wide-aperture sensor array.

The SR-71 was now locked into the Flanker's battle management system. This time Magadan would not fail to either bring the Blackbird down to earth or blow it completely out of the skies.

Cox said, "Uh-oh," as the threat icon materialized on the SR's AN/APG-67 radar scope set on track-while-scan. Immediately the black stealth ship was shunted from automatic pilot to Cox's direct hands-on control.

Expectations had now been confirmed. Cox had no

doubt regarding what lay in store. It would be a race to outrun the Russian fighter plane.

Using the full afterburner power of the SR's twin turbo ramjets to now propel the Blackbird upward and toward home base at maximum thrust, Cox kept his eyes riveted on the cockpit's radar scope.

Unlike the previous encounter with a hostile jet, the Russian fighter was staying glued to the Blackbird's tail with bulldoglike tenacity.

Cox pushed the SR-71 to the limits of its performance envelope, using every possible tactic to squeeze maximum velocity and altitude from the agile black plane.

But the Russian fighter continued to stay on the SR's tail.

It continued to pursue the Blackbird relentlessly.

Having failed to outdistance the intercepter, Cox decided to try an oppositional technique.

He was aware that the Russian aircraft was capable of attaining flight speeds of Mach 3 and better, which made it at least as fast as the American spyplane. However, the Flanker's very ability to pull high Mach numbers would be the means by which Cox hoped to evade pursuit.

Suddenly applying the SR's air brake, Cox slowed the Blackbird's speed to the point where she was virtually standing still in the sky, a maneuver that was highly dangerous because of its potential to produce a flameout condition.

The Russian pilot saw the maneuver and grasped what his adversary had in mind, quickly applying his own air brakes in response, but he knew that he had been outfoxed again by the wily American pilot.

Unable to stop in time at the high speeds it was traveling, the Russian fighter shot past the virtually stationary SR-71 at velocities exceeding those of an artillery shell.

As soon as Cox saw the Sukhoi hurtle past the cockpit of the Blackbird, he throttled up and sped the spyplane high into the stratosphere on full afterburner.

At the rate it was traveling, the Russian fighter overshot the SR-71's position like a streak of greased lightning. Within seconds it was several miles from the Blackbird's last position.

By this time, Cox had sent the spyplane into a steep pull-up and rocketed high into the sky, increasing the distance between them by an even greater margin.

Magadan cursed as he saw the blip on his screen fade and then quickly disappear. Turning in the sky and finetuning his equipment, he was nevertheless unable to pick up the target signature.

"I've lost the target aircraft," he radioed to the TU-126. "Do you see it anywhere?"

Borovich was already by the chief R/O's radar installation, his cold gray eyes locked on the screen with its glowing yellow, green and red target icons highlighted against a blue background, the scanning quadrant signified by a shifting pie slice of lighter blue that circuited the screen every thirty seconds, constantly refreshing the computer-enhanced FLAT JACK radar telemetry.

"No, we ..." he began, then, "... *yes*, Magadan. We've picked it up again!" Borovich excitedly read off the new coordinates, marveling afresh at the skill of the American pilot.

He had cleverly angled the craft several miles to the northeast of his original course and then swiftly plunged her down from an altitude of sixty-three thousand feet to one which brought the plane coasting low over the mountains on a radar-evading course heading, an attempt on the American's part to fly under the curtain and to trade off speed for stealth.

Incredible flying, Borovich thought to himself as he concluded his transmission to Magadan, then punched in a series of keystrokes which called up two other fighters on patrol in the general area.

Magadan had screwed up twice already, and at any rate, the fighter pilot had no right to consider Commonwealth airspace as his private hunting preserve.

The Sukhoi flier needed help in order to catch the elusive Blackbird. And Magadan would receive that help, whether he liked it or not.

19

For a few minutes, Cox thought they might have a shot at making it. He knew, though, that the game was ultimately zero sum.

With Russian AWACS' over-the-horizon backscatter radar able to track a wide area and deliver highly accurate targeting coordinates to the agile Russian fighters, there was no way that the Blackbird would not be picked up again.

The next contact took place quickly.

At once the SR-71's long-range radar flashed the threat icon of the pursuing Flanker on the navigational screen to the left of Cox.

His jaw tensed, Cox skimmed the Blackbird lower, aware that the maneuver would inhibit the ability of radar to accurately track the plane, but also knowing that this tactic would not in itself be enough to ensure survival.

Convinced soon thereafter that the Sukhoi was locked on the SR's target signature, Cox gained altitude. His navigational screen showed that he was now not far from the Russian coast.

Another few minutes of flight time and he might make it out of Commonwealth airspace entirely. However, radar was also showing that he was now within range of the Flanker's AA-ALAMO 10 rockets.

The Flanker was closing fast, now at a distance of

sixty miles but eating up the sky lying between them with a vengeance. At the supersonic speeds of the chase, the Russian fighter plane would soon be right on top of the SR.

Suddenly two more icons appeared on the SR's radar screen. Cox realized to his chagrin that these represented two more Russian fighter planes, closing fast at twelve o'clock.

Now the excrement had really hit the whirling blades, thought Cox.

The Blackbird was caught between a flock of hungry sky eagles that were pursuing it with a vengeance.

Cox's thoughts turned to the single piece of ordnance carried on board the plane, the long-range Highwire ALCM. But the brilliant, terminally guided antiaircraft missile round would only be successful in taking out one of the fighters, leaving the spyplane vulnerable against the other two aircraft.

Cox decided not to deploy Highwire just yet; there would be little point in taking such action now.

Just then he made visual contact with the two Russian jets vectoring toward the Blackbird. They were Flankers, powerful and fast, bristling with the most sophisticated rockets in the AA class.

The warplanes had sighted the Blackbird too.

They were wiggling their wings in the international code, signaling him to land the black stealth ship as they shot past the Blackbird and yawed hard to port and starboard, buffeting the SR with the fierce turbulence of their combined jetwash.

Cox knew that this would be the last warning of its kind that he was likely to receive.

The next communication would be in the form of a burst of 23 mm cannon fire across the Blackbird's chined nose assembly. More than likely, the opposition would shoot to knock the spyplane out of the sky.

As the two attack planes reconverged, Cox could not hear the angry colloquy taking place between their two pilots and Magadan, who was closing fast at a six o'clock bearing.

"What the hell are you doing here?" Magadan asked the other pilots. "The aircraft is mine. I get first crack at her."

"You're crazy, comrade," one of the two pilots replied. "We have our orders and they come directly from MOSS: we're to assist you in bringing down the intruder aircraft."

"Very well," Magadan growled, aware that he could not countermand the orders.

He would give Borovich a piece of his mind when he saw him, ranking officer or not. He should not have been co-opted in his pursuit of the American plane.

Magadan was still several miles from the Blackbird and would not reach the target's position for a few minutes yet. He feared that by the time he reached the airspace, the plane would already have been brought down, in pieces or otherwise, by the recent arrivals to the fight.

Cox, meanwhile, slowed the Blackbird and nosed her down toward the ground, apparently in compliance with the orders to land.

The two Flankers were now flying abeam of him, on either side of the Blackbird, herding him between them like two ranchers on horseback corralling a runaway bull.

Cox had one desperate gambit left in his bag of tricks and he knew that now was the time to play out his hand.

Suddenly applying full thrust while at the same time pulling back on the stick, he sent the SR catapulting skyward in a completely unexpected, tight pull-up maneuver which caught the flanking Russians totally by surprise.

The two hostile warplanes fired their 23 mm cannons at the escaping SR, but Cox had already jinked the Blackbird hard to one side, having anticipated the reactions of the Flanker pilots.

Instead of striking the fast-flying Blackbird, the heavy-caliber tracer rounds shot by the Sukhois crisscrossed through space.

Fratricide was the result.

As rounds from the leftmost Flanker walloped into the fuselage of the other jet, the plane exploded suddenly into a ball of fire.

Perilously close to the stricken aircraft, the pilot of the first Sukhoi could not evade the rapidly whirling fragments of the burning Flanker, which scythed through the air like shrapnel from a burst of flak.

A time-tick later, white-hot wreckage splinters ripped into the hull of the second jet and smashed their way into the plane's fuel tanks, igniting them instantly. The mortally wounded pilot screamed in agony as the Flanker exploded into a second fireball, but he managed to eject from the cockpit by conditioned reflex.

What was propelled through the open cockpit hatch by the rocket-propelled ejector seat, however, was a burning human firebrand doused with aviation fuel and spinning through blue space like an animate Roman candle.

Magadan couldn't believe his eyes as he now approached the kill zone in the sky.

The Russian pilot was horrified.

The American flier had eluded the two Flanker aircraft and destroyed all personnel in a stunning display of aerobatics. He would not prove so fortunate again, Magadan promised himself.

His strategem would not work against a single aircraft, and not against Magadan. Although he was eager to avenge the deaths of the pilots by killing the SR, his instructions were to bring down the plane and destroy it only as a final resort.

He would follow those orders to the letter. Magadan was a professional.

Deploying the Sukhoi's wing strake-mounted 23 mm cannon, Magadan fired a warning burst of tracer rounds across the Blackbird's wings, then sped the Flanker laterally across the SR's flight path to indicate that he possessed complete air superiority.

Seeing the glowing tracers speed past the cockpit and correctly interpreting the maneuvers of the Sukhoi, Cox knew that he was outmatched by the more maneuverable and heavily armed jet fighter.

He could not risk using the Highwire ALCM at such close range, and besides this, the SR's long-range radar showed that more jets were even now being scrambled on intercept vectors.

Despite the certainty of capture and imprisonment, both Cox and Gilroy would die if the SR remained airborne, prey to the flock of hungry eagles that sought to rip her apart in midair.

Only a single alternative to destruction now presented itself.

Cox would have to land the SR.

He nosed the Blackbird toward the ground, which grew larger in his visual field with each passing second.

There!

Cox sighted the stretch of highway that ran ruler-straight through a mountain valley below. Eyeballing the straightaway indicated that its length would suffice to enable him to safely land the SR-71.

Minutes later, the Blackbird's landing gear screeched against tarmac as the plane made a rough landing on the blacktop highway, its drag chute trailing behind it.

Cox and Gilroy undogged their cockpit hatches and hoisted themselves into positions where they could watch the sky. Up in the air above, Magadan circled them warily, firing a burst of autocannon fire to let the downed fliers know that he was riding herd on them.

He had already radioed MOSS, which had in turn contacted a military base nearby, and ground troops were already being deployed. Cox held up his hands and pointed down to the asphalt with one hand, indicating to the circling fighter that he and Gilroy were going to climb down from the SR.

The Flanker screamed overhead but did not fire its guns, indicating to Cox that they would not be prevented from leaving the plane. But in Magadan's confidence lay the seeds of a disastrous error.

Waiting until just before the Flanker banked sharply to begin a tight turn that would bring it back overhead at an angle that, for a few seconds, would obscure the pilot's line of sight behind the fuselage of the SR-71, Cox hollered at Gilroy to run for the cover of an outcropping of boulders situated beside the highway and just beyond the grounded plane.

Cox had deliberately pulled the nose assembly of the SR-71 as close to the outcropping as he could on landing, anticipating the possibility of escape.

Magadan saw the two figures, who had shucked off their bulky flight suits, break toward the jumbled rocks and cursed his stupidity for allowing them to leave the SR's cockpits. His finger hovered over the fire control button on his joystick, but he dared not shoot.

To do so from this angle would almost certainly blow up the plane. If he did so, the Americans might still escape and he would surely face severe disciplinary measures from his superiors. Magadan held his fire and on his next pass saw that the Americans had vanished from sight into the dense woods that began just beyond the highway.

Still, it did not matter for the present that his quarry had escaped. Magadan told himself that the only matter of importance now was that the Blackbird was down. As for the Americans, they could not get very far on the ground.

In a very short time, the entire sector would become the target of an intensive manhunt, one from which the two downed aviators had no chance of escaping.

20

Svalbard Island

Darkness had fallen by the time Holloway issued the order for the KC-135Q refueling planes to extract from their loiter zones and return at once to the Watchtower mission-support facility.

Electronic interception of air-to-air radio traffic between the deployed Russian fighters and MOSS had indicated that the Russians had identified the SR-71 in their airspace, and since several hours had elapsed without any sign of the Blackbird, Holloway was forced to assume that the spyplane had been shot down by Russian interceptor aircraft.

As Holloway scanned the radar display, hoping against hope that Cox and Gilroy would somehow return to Svalbard, he knew that his optimism was based as much on a refusal to accept reality as on the guilt he felt for sending the Watchtower air crew out on a suicide mission, and the higher good it served for the moment be darned.

Holloway willed the icon representing the SR's radar signature to flash on the screen with the suddenness of redemption.

But it did not, because it could not: the plane was simply not there anymore. It had vanished from the skies.

Finally giving in to the inevitable, the mission director issued instructions for a watch to be kept on the radar probes and emergency channels to be constantly scanned.

For the present, Holloway had other business to take care of. Picking up the phone, he notified the NSA mission director aboard the Glover-class frigate and informed him that the SR-71 had failed to return to base and was presumed lost.

Holloway was assured by the mission director that the President would be immediately informed and was asked to keep the NSA honcho up-to-date on any further developments. Holloway promised that he would do so and terminated the transmission.

The knowledge that the crew of the SR-71 had been expendable did not help matters any or ease the burden of guilt which Holloway felt. The Watchtower mission manager walked dejectedly past the C^3 crew without meeting any of their eyes and trudged out of the Quonset hut into the cold drizzle that fell from overcast skies.

Holloway felt the icy needles sting his face as he stared out across the ocean toward the Russian coast beyond the choppy waters, and he cursed the nothingness that he saw on the empty gray horizon.

Eastern Russian Republic, C.I.S.

The vasaltnicki team neared the outskirts of the village of Gody Nimovka, in the vicinity of the base that was their destination. They had been moving by night and by day, covering as much ground as possible in order to avoid detection by search units that were hunting them.

Those teams had been sent out after Tallin's men in the aftermath of the confrontation with the militia patrol two days before. In the interim, the strike team had on at least one occasion come perilously close to interception by another armed patrol.

Unlike the previous engagement, which had ended in bloodshed, they had this time succeeded in evading the patrol and had not encountered hostile forces since that initial confrontation.

Tallin knew that his men were tired; in fact, that they had reached the limits of physical exhaustion and would benefit from the opportunity to rest and eat a decent meal in the village.

The villagers in this area were no friends of the Center, Tallin knew, nor even of the republic per se, and he weighed the dangers of exposure against the potential benefits of commanding a well-fed and rested unit in the culminating phase of the operation.

He decided finally to send Piotr and Gennady into the village to test the waters. The rest of his men would secure a remain-overnight position not far from the village site.

Roughly an hour later, Piotr and Gennady returned to the team's temporary bivouac in the company of a man dressed in rough peasant's clothes.

His head was covered with the peaked workman's cap and he wore the *kosovorotka*—a side-vented, upright-collared shirt—beneath a sheepskin coat in the manner of the *bedniaks,* or peasant farmers, of the hill country, and his face bore the strong Tartar features of the inhabitants of the wild and desolate region.

His age was indeterminate, for the severe stress of life in the high mountain passes of the central region wrinkles the skin and dulls the mind at an early age.

The peasant introduced himself as Rudenko and told Tallin that he was the village chieftain. He welcomed the vasaltnickis and invited the warriors to spend the night at his *piatestenka*, where he related that his wife was already preparing a hot supper for them.

Piotr helped clarify the story which Rudenko had told him earlier. There had been strange goings-on for the better part of a year in the vicinity of the mountain village. Young men from the hamlet had been rounded up by armed soldiers and taken away to work high in the mountains.

None of those who had left had yet returned.

For the past few months, truck convoys had been arriving in the vicinity with steadily increasing regularity, and large planes had been sighted taking off and landing with great frequency, frightening the villagers, who seldom heard the rumble of modern jet engines and had never known the savage thunder which the powerful thrusters of these large planes produced.

Soldiers had sworn to burn the village and kill its inhabitants, Rudenko said further, if a word was spoken to outsiders regarding the goings-on.

The villagers had been frightened into cowed silence. They had no doubt that the soldiers would carry out their threat. Terrorized into acquiescence, they had mutely kept their uneasy peace.

Until now, that is.

Upon learning that an armed commando force had come to the village with the base as its target, Rudenko had called together the leading members of the community for a *skhod*, or council meeting, and hastily voted as to whether or not to extend the men their hospitality.

The extra time needed to reach the decision had accounted for the lateness of Piotr and Gennady's return to the RON site. However, the wait was worth having gone through, because the village elders had in the end voted to take the armed men into their confidence.

Within a half hour, the vasaltnicki team was squatting cross-legged on the dirt floor of a *piatestenka*, the traditional peasant's two-room cottage heated by a crude fireplace built of mortared, irregularly shaped stones.

The men were sitting down to the first hot meal they had consumed in many days, and enjoying every mouthful. While they messed, Rudenko introduced the commandos to the other men with whom he had conferred, and Tallin received more information regarding the secret base that was the team's objective.

Spreading out one of the military sector maps he had brought with him, Tallin asked the men to identify the rough location of the base.

"Here," Rudenko said, tapping a stubby brown finger on the exact location that the captured sector map from the militia patrol had indicated.

Tallin cast a knowing glance at Gennady and Piotr, who had closely followed the exchange.

"Have any of your people actually visited the installation?" Tallin asked Rudenko through the medium of Mikhail, who translated his Moscow Russian into the local mountain dialect.

"Yes," Mikhail said while Rudenko nodded. "Several times, in fact. He says that if you like, he can recommend an expert guide who will take us to a site where we can reconnoiter the base with reasonable safety."

"Is it one of the men here?" Tallin asked, looking around the room at the other peasants, who stood on the periphery of the discussion.

"No," Mikhail replied a few minutes later, "but he can be brought here if you desire."

Tallin did indeed desire to meet the guide who Rudenko had said was available, and one of the men standing near the doorway of the hut was immediately sent off to fetch him.

After about fifteen minutes and several more cups of

hot buttered tea, the guide arrived. Tallin saw the young man come into the stone hut and crouch beside him.

"They have told me you need a guide," he said in Russian with a Moscow accent. "I'm your man."

"You speak like a Muscovite," Tallin replied with surprise. "How is this?"

"I studied medicine at Moscow University," he replied. "I am the village doctor and, quite apart from the fact that my two brothers were taken away to labor at the base you seek to destroy, I am angry at those who have invaded our village.

"What Rudenko says is true. I can take you to the base. I can use a weapon too, if you have one available."

Tallin smiled at the young man whose earnest features bespoke his conviction and courage.

"Come and join us," he told the doctor. "But you had better be prepared for a long night. We'll want to see the base before first light, and there will be a lot of planning to do before then. What's your name?"

"I am called Barsov," the doctor returned.

21

Istra, Russian Republic, C.I.S.

Bordering on anarchy, the Russian Republic was in an upheaval of revolt. The massive civil disorder which prevailed had forced Russian President Sergei Pavlovich to follow protocols intended to protect the Russian leader in time of nuclear war.

The underground bunker system was extensive, hardened against N-EMP and capable of withstanding all levels of attack apart from a direct hit by a one-megaton nuclear warhead.

Pavlovich now sat in his inner office.

He had summoned Samsonov to keep him posted on the progress of the back-channel operation which had been intended to bring to a halt the snowballing of the nation toward anarchy. Russia was a tinderbox awaiting a spark to set it off, and Pavlovich knew that the covert base in the central region was the flint which would produce that fatal spark.

His instincts were to crush the rebellion with a massive air-land assault, bomb it to rubble, then send in ground forces to mop up.

Yet Pavlovich also knew that he could not afford to take this direct course for fear of sending the wrong signals to both his own people and the rest of the world.

He was like a man standing on the ledge of a burning building: afraid to jump and not foolish enough to go back inside.

"You promised me results," the President said to Samsonov. "When will I see these results? Believe me, Valery Ivan'ch, I cannot afford to wait much longer. I must act soon."

"You may not like what I have to tell you," Samsonov said. "But it is news of great importance."

"What is it?" Pavlovich asked with sudden eagerness.

"Something that I believe is central to an understanding of the crisis," Samsonov returned. "We have evidence that the rioting in the central region was instigated by Black Beret forces sent by a single man."

"Who?" asked the President in consternation.

"General Fyodor Aleksiev," Samsonov said. "I am certain the name rings a bell."

"Of course it does," Pavlovich replied. "Who has not heard of Aleksiev?"

"Precisely," Samsonov said with a smile. "Who indeed has not? Aleksiev was one of the heroes of the war in Afghanistan. He is a man of immense popularity."

"And, as commander in chief of the Strategic Rocket Forces, is second only to myself in responsibility for the deployment of nuclear weapons."

"Also correct," Samsonov replied. "Unfortunately, my friend, he may also be the catalyst behind the current crisis."

"What are you saying?" the President asked, not believing what he had just heard. "How can this be as you claim?"

"It is a simple matter, really," Samsonov answered with characteristic sangfroid. "Aleksiev commands tremendous loyalty. He is able to pull strings which nobody else can. In some respects his power transcends even yours, if I may be permitted to say so."

"I still am at a loss to understand, Valery Ivan'ch." The President spoke perplexedly. "Even if one of the former Soviet Union's greatest military heroes was bent on bringing about a coup d'état, how could he be responsible for what you accuse him of?"

"Quite simply, Aleksiev has, over the course of the last two years, embarked on an ambitious project to create a military power base in the heart of Russia," said Samsonov. "By manipulating computer manifests, he has caused a secret base to be built in the mountains of the north central region, complete with a battalion of troops and two Blackjack bombers fully loaded with nuclear cruise missiles."

"This is staggering news!" exclaimed the President. "I can't believe it!"

"You must," Samsonov insisted. "The evidence against the general is irrefutable."

He took from his briefcase a bound report and handed it to the President. "Leaf through this document," Samsonov went on. "It is all here. Photographic reproductions as well are included. It will make a believer out of you."

The President went around to his desk. Putting on his glasses, he sat and leafed through the pages of the report as Samsonov had suggested, lingering for long minutes as he reread several pages. His head began to swim at the revelations contained within the laser-printed sheets, many bearing corroborative charts and photographic illustrations which seemed to show beyond all question that what Samsonov had claimed was the truth.

"The KGB must have received reports," Pavlovich said in a tone conveying horror and astonishment. "There must have been orbital surveillance data," he added as the magnitude of the undertaking became clearer.

"Aleksiev adroitly suppressed all evidence of his treachery," Samsonov explained. "He had established a network of accomplices everywhere. They are, however, being rounded up even as we speak. Quietly, of course, you understand."

"But the base," the President suddenly ventured as a warning bell sounded in his mind. "Tallin's group cannot be enough. Surely we must send in a larger force to seize control of the stronghold."

"No, Sergei Grigor'ch," Samsonov said, shaking his head. "That we cannot possibly afford to do. What little faith in your ability to govern the nation which remains in the public mind would be undermined beyond all hope of salvation. The base must be destroyed without any possibility of the secret leaking. No, my friend: now more than ever, Tallin is our only hope."

The President took off his glasses and rubbed his eyes with his fingers. When he looked back at Samsonov again, there was resolution etched on his face.

"I suppose you are right," he declared. "Which leads me to ask if there is any recent news of the vasaltnickis."

"There is," Samsonov responded, brightening somewhat. "They are near their target. They will strike soon."

"I only hope it is soon enough," the President exclaimed, and tossed his glasses atop the desk. "May God be with them."

Washington, D.C.

The black limo carrying President Webster Bancroft to Andrews Air Force Base was constructed of a laminated fiberglass-Kevlar composite which was resistant to small-arms hits and explosive splinter burst.

Its tinted, blastproof windows would not be penetrated by anything less than a proximate strike by a high-explosive antitank round, and its tires were run-flat, filled with a silicon-based mixture which made them impervious to blowouts.

Inside the limo, the U.S. President was preoccupied with somber thoughts. This was a day he had dreaded since taking office, a dread which had been dissipated by recent events but which had now come back with a vengeance to grip his soul with a numbing coldness.

War clouds loomed on the horizon.

Under an escort of Secret Service personnel in unmarked cars in front and behind the President's limo, the Chief Executive was being hustled to a plane which stood warming up on the tarmac under provisions of JEEP, the Joint Emergency Evacuation Plan implemented in time of grave national military crisis.

It was not Air Force One, but another plane, the "doomsday plane" bearing the code name NEACP, an acronym which stood for the National Emergency Airborne Command Post.

NEACP, or "Kneecap," by which the aircraft was usually known, was a USAF E-4. Standing ready on a twenty-four-hour basis, the plane is intended to become airborne in wartime, bearing the President and his senior military and civilian advisors to the comparative safety of the air.

Its fuselage crammed with sophisticated command, control and communications gear, Kneecap is manned by the Joint Chiefs of Staff, all of whom were already on board the aircraft as the President's limo raced through the gates of Andrews and sped onto the runway tarmac.

Bancroft saw the E-4 plane just ahead of him and waited until the Secret Service escorts had left their cars.

While they covered his exit from the limo with an assortment of automatic assault weaponry, the President walked up the boarding stairs and entered the plane, clutching the attaché case containing the Gold Codes: activation codes for America's nuclear arsenal.

Inside, he saw that the JCS were all present, their faces somber as he greeted them and went aft to his cabin to check on the First Lady.

Within minutes after the President's arrival, Kneecap rolled down the taxiway and was soon airborne. In minutes it had climbed to its cruising altitude of thirty-five thousand feet and was flying above the level of the clouds.

The President sat down at the conference table in Kneecap's situation room, surrounded by his advisors. The evidence before him was irrefutable. The Watchtower mission was now terminated because the SR-71 spyplane had failed to return to Svalbard.

However, the intelligence that the crew of the Blackbird had been able to gather before they had been downed by the Russians clearly demonstrated that nuclear warheads had been stockpiled at a secluded base and were being prepped for delivery to targets inside the United States.

Bancroft had spoken via the hot line to the Russian President, who had denied all knowledge of the threat. Yet the President could not afford to take the Russian leader's glib reassurances at face value. Pavlovich knew a great deal more than he was telling, and this did not bode well.

Not when the hard data which he had in front of him—intelligence which had been gained at the cost of the crew of the Watchtower spy aircraft—proved incontrovertibly that nuclear arms were being readied for a surgical strike.

This was no Cuban missile crisis either, the President lamented. Had it been so, there would have been room for negotiation, pressure to be applied, leverage to be used.

Unlike that earlier U.S.-Soviet confrontation, this present one had been generated by an unknown quantity, a rogue commander who had placed himself beyond the mechanisms of control by the Russian central government in Moscow.

Why had not Pavlovich moved to oust the commander? wondered the President. He knew that any attempt to dislodge him would prove to be a tricky affair, since the renegade could get his planes airborne and into cruise-missile launch range within a very brief time.

Pavlovich either was stalling for time or had given up entirely. If the former was true, there might still be hope to avert a global confrontation with dire ramifications. If the Russians could clean their own sheets and neutralize the threat, the crisis might disappear of its own accord.

But there was no way to be sure of this happening. U.S. strategic nuclear forces had been readied. The President wished that deployment of his "thin" SDI missile shield was already in place, but it was not.

Despite everything they could do, a single countervalue strike on a U.S. target by a Russian warhead would precipitate a nuclear crisis that might escalate rapidly into a full-scale exchange.

Mutually assured destruction loomed on the horizon, more so now than at any other time in history. A Cold War had been fought and won by the West. The coming hot war would have no winners.

22

Eastern Russian Republic, C.I.S.

The two-and-a-half-ton military transport trucks arrived at the landing site, stopping short just behind the stationary spyplane.

Colonel Yevgeny Nosenko ordered his men to deploy but not to approach in close proximity to the downed SR until a demolition crew had gotten a chance to go over it, ensuring that its fuselage and cockpit had not been booby-trapped.

Nosenko smoked a cigarette as he watched the two-man demolition team subject the daggerlike aircraft to a series of electronic sweeps, then carefully subject its sleek, chined fuselage to a close-up inspection.

Once these procedures had been carried out to their complete satisfaction, one of the two demolition officers set up a metal stepladder beside the cockpit and, after scrutinizing the interior of the cockpit with an electronic scanner, climbed in himself.

Both inspectors now pronounced the aircraft free from booby traps and returned to their vehicle.

"She's clean, sir," one of the two demo men reported to the colonel. "It's okay to haul her away. Beautiful plane, isn't she, sir?"

"Indeed she is," Nosenko replied to the man who had spoken. "Remain here in case you're needed further."

"Yes, sir," the officer responded crisply.

Nosenko then unclipped a compact radio transceiver unit from his belt and depressed the send button on the hand-held communications device. The transport vehicle with its long, flat bed was standing by, having arrived just behind the troop transports. A platoon of army engineers had arrived too, with a heavy crane in tow, behind the vehicle.

"Gaff the plane and load it onto the truck." Nosenko spoke into the mouthpiece of the transceiver, relaying his orders to the sergeant who was in charge of the engineer crew. "You know where to take the aircraft."

"Yes, sir," the crew chief replied to the colonel's instructions.

He then relayed a variation of those orders to his own men, instructing them to stand by as he radioed the crane operators to rig the plane so that it could be lifted up and set on the bed of the truck.

Nosenko watched as the crane crew proceeded to rig the Blackbird for transloading onto the flatbed vehicle. Assuring himself that the loading operation had been initiated properly and that it was progressing smoothly, the colonel next turned his attention to the problem concerning capture of the escaped American crew of the SR-71.

The two fliers reported to have run from the plane on landing were nowhere in the vicinity. According to the brief filed by the fighter pilot who had forced down the spyplane, they had succeeded in making a desperate, albeit successful, break for freedom just after the American photoreconnaissance aircraft had been made to land.

They could not have gotten very far, however, and the colonel did not anticipate very much of a problem in apprehending the fleeing Americans. Without assistance, they would not be able to survive for long in this inhospitable mountain terrain, especially on foot. Capturing them was essentially a matter of time and diligence, and Nosenko had both in sufficient quantities to ensure ultimate success.

"Deploy your men," he shouted at the captain in charge of the company of Russian ground troops which had been trucked to the landing site to act as a search party for the Americans. "Have them scour the area and bring the captives back here. Coordinate with the helicopter crew when the chopper arrives."

"Yes, sir," the captain responded with a crisp salute, and shouted orders at his subordinates, who began to jump from the rear of the canvas-covered, heavy transport trucks.

Soon the air became filled with the sudden clatter of boot leather against tarmac as the Russian ground troops started to fan out to the north of the highway strip, the direction in which the Americans were reported as having last been seen.

The troops carried Krinkov short-barreled AKR assault rifles and knew that they were expected to use their weapons to wound rather than kill, if at all possible. The Americans were wanted for interrogation and were more valuable alive, at this point, than they were dead.

As the troops fanned out, they soon heard an increasingly loud roar building overhead to an earsplitting crescendo and moments later could make out the bulky silhouette of an Mi8 HiP-4 helicopter as the heavy rotorcraft took shape above the treeline.

The HiP would scan the area from the air while the troops searched on the ground, and the colonel had no doubt that the Americans would soon be taken into custody.

He put away the transceiver unit and lit another cigarette while he watched the engineer crew make ready to tow the Blackbird away, thinking that yes, this was indeed a beautiful aircraft.

The cave was well screened from the terrain surrounding the mountainside by a thicket of trees and dense undergrowth. Cox and Gilroy had found the hide site while running from the plane and taken shelter in it the previous afternoon.

Night had fallen.

They had eaten emergency MREs, the military meals, ready to eat, which had been part of their emergency kit. Cox now stood the first watch, his P-90 close-assault weapon lying on the dusty floor of the cave within quick reach.

Deeper inside the cave, stretched out on its cold stone floor, Air Force Lieutenant Amanda Gilroy lay wide awake. She could not sleep but was trying to get some rest before her turn at watch came up in a few more hours.

Gilroy's thoughts turned inexplicably back to her years in high school in Marshalltown, Iowa. In extraordinary detail, recollections of former classmates and experiences they had shared together swam up before her drowsy mind's eye with crystal clarity as she recalled memories that had been long forgotten.

She drifted off into an uneasy sleep, reassuring herself that this mental phenomenon was a common reaction to conditions of high stress and that she would be all right, that everything would work out all right. . . .

Gilroy woke up with a start in what seemed a moment later. She consulted her watch and realized that she had actually been asleep for several hours.

It was almost dawn now, and time to relieve Cox at his sentry post. Taking her P-90, she went groggily to the cave mouth and saw Cox's silhouette against the lighter blackness of the night sky.

"My turn at watch," she told him.

"Go back to sleep," he responded gruffly, staring off into the predawn darkness.

"You're tired and it's my turn," Gilroy told the older man. "Now get in there."

Cox turned and nodded with resignation.

He did indeed feel tired.

"Don't worry, kid," he said, squeezing Gilroy's shoulder as he trudged back inside the cavern with heavy steps. "We'll make it."

"I doubt it," Gilroy returned as she sat on the cold stones of the cave and rested her weapon across her knees. "But thanks for saying so anyway, boss."

It was daybreak when Cox was awakened by Gilroy. As his mind cleared, he told her that they had to move as they had planned to do earlier. They had stayed in their remain-overnight position long enough.

They could not afford to stay in a stationary position for too long, because the risk of detection would increase with every passing hour spent there.

In the turmoil which now swept like wildfire across the Russian Republic, a slim chance existed that Cox and Gilroy could make contact with local militia units whose sympathies would not lie with Moscow and which might believe that making overtures to the West would be to their advantage.

As it happened, events overtook Cox and Gilroy far too quickly, and they were denied the chance to exercise even this desperate option. They had remained too long in the hide site: those forces that sought them had finally reached their position.

Search team one caught sight of the Americans as they descended the sloping banks of the steep gully.

"We've found the two escaped crewmen," the team's leader radioed to the pilot of the search chopper.

"They're about two kilometers north of the landing position on the road."

"Roger," the HiP pilot replied. "We are on our way. Keep the Americans in sight. Out."

Minutes later, Cox heard the earsplitting din made by four powerful rotorblades revolving at high speeds as the HiP hovered overhead. The translator who sat in the chopper's jump seat picked up the radio mike and set the unit on public address.

"Give yourselves up," he called out in English, his amplified voice audible above the roar of the HiP's whirling rotorblades. "You are completely surrounded. If you fail to surrender, you will be apprehended by force. You have five minutes to make up your mind."

Cox told Gilroy to make a break for it. He would draw the search team's fire. With luck, she might still manage to escape.

"There's no point," she answered him without even having to pause to consider. "Where would I go?"

"Yeah, you're right, kid," Cox replied resignedly. What was the sense? They were trapped in the middle of nowhere anyway. "Like the saying goes, 'Somehow I don't think we're in Kansas anymore.' "

Cox dropped his P-90 CAW to the ground and held up his hands and Gilroy did the same where they had stopped on the slope just below the cavern entrance.

As the amplified voice of the English-speaking soldier in the HiP chopper boomed down from over their heads and warned the prisoners to remain still, Cox and Gilroy helplessly watched the squads of greatcoat-clad Russian troops running toward them.

PART THREE

Fratricide

23

With the villager named Barsov acting as guide, the vasaltnicki team ascended the mountain heights.

Tallin had spent most of the previous night pumping the villagers for every scrap of information regarding the base that they could provide him. He had not been disappointed and felt certain that Barsov would be effective in bringing the unit to the base.

While he had been debriefing Barsov and the rest of the village elite, the men of the vasaltnicki team had been resting and cleaning their weapons.

Each was now at the peak of readiness.

The men and the implements of war which they carried were mission-capable.

Now, at 0420 hours, the full moon had set behind the tops of the Siberian pines an hour before and the horizon was faintly lit by the glow of false dawn.

The treetops rustled overhead and a cold breeze blew down from the snowcapped mountaintops which towered above them, the soughing of the wind broken every so often by the eerie howling of wild wolves that inhabited the steppes.

The commando unit moved slowly and cautiously, the eyes of each man scanning the terrain ahead, his weapon cradled in his arms, aware that he had come to the end of his trek and to the beginning of his battle.

For his own part, Tallin welcomed the chance to finally get into a real scrap. Twenty-two months in a stinking prison cell at Lefortovo had been the worst experience of his life, far worse than any privation he had suffered in combat.

His body and soul both ached for action, and the prospect of being in a fight again made his pulse quicken and his senses come to life in a way that no other form of activity had ever been able to accomplish.

Combat alone could exhilarate him in such a manner.

Tallin suspected that the rest of the men in the team felt the same way as he did. The years spent in Afghanistan had conditioned them all to crave the adrenaline high of fighting.

Out of all the other unit personnel, only Piotr and Gennady had communicated these feelings to Tallin. He was certain, however, that each and every one of them was eager to put his abilities to the test. A veteran fighter grew to wonder if he still had what it took after a while.

Despite the dangers of combat, Tallin well understood that one of the greatest joys of life was to be found in the baptism of one's manhood in the blooding of battle, and that the need for this timeless ritual was one which could never be wholly taken from the human spirit.

In time, Barsov gestured for the team to come to a halt, after about forty minutes of steady climbing over a mountain trail which led up through a dense pine forest. Seeing the village guide motioning for Tallin to join him, Tallin moved in a crouch toward the head of the column from his position at the rear element and hunkered down beside the villager.

"What is it?" he asked.

"Motorized patrol," the guide whispered. "Down there."

Tallin took night-observation binoculars from the

side pocket of his forest-camouflage-pattern parka and looked down at the mountain road, which lay about twenty meters below the shallow slope angling down from the higher ground the team occupied.

He saw a Russian army staff car manned by a trio of greatcoated infantry soldiers.

Mounted to the rear of the cab was an NSV 12.70 mm heavy machine gun, a type of weapon that the former Spetsnaz troops were familiar with from their tours of Afghanistan. The greatcoat-clad team was shouldering AK-47 rifles, and two of them stood by idly smoking while the third man relieved himself against a tree.

Piotr had slid up soundlessly beside Tallin, and after he'd had his look at the patrol, Tallin passed his trusted lieutenant the night-vision-capable field glasses.

"Do we take them?" Piotr asked as he scanned the scene below with the light-amplifying binoculars.

"No," the unit commander said with a shake of his head, deciding that engaging in a skirmish was not at all what they needed now. "We'll give them ten minutes more. If they aren't on their way by then, we'll hit them, but not until."

In roughly five minutes, the three soldiers climbed back into the staff car.

The slamming of doors echoed through the predawn stillness; then the motor roared to life as the driver turned the key in the vehicle's ignition and ground off in low gear along the dirt road, red taillights finally winking off as the staff car disappeared around a tight bend in the mountain roadway a few moments later.

Tallin waited until the operations zone was completely silent again, except for the soughing sound of the wind and the rustling of leaves. Then, with a nod to Barsov, he signaled that the strike team was ready to advance again.

Barsov had the team follow the road for half a mile, then cut up into the woods to one side at a sharp angle. The terrain was rockier here and the stands of mountain pines and fir had by now thinned out to a fraction of their density at the lower altitudes from which the vasaltnickis had first begun their march.

About a half hour of slow but steady ascent later, Barsov again called the team to a halt.

"There, below us, lies the base I spoke of," he told Tallin, pointing ahead to the edge of the land, beyond which stretched the deep magenta-and-gray colors of a predawn sky.

Tallin crouch-walked his way to the edge of the high ground and looked down. Adjusted to the darkness, his naked eyes had no difficulty in discerning the camp lying directly below them, on the near side of a large mountain valley.

The black, straight line of a runway easily long and wide enough to accommodate heavy bombers dominated the scene below. Three smaller black strips running perpendicular to the runway on the side nearest to Tallin were taxiways, and lined up in between them appeared to be the shapes of fighter planes covered with camouflage tarp.

The main compound of the base was a large area roughly a third of the runway's length, situated on the same side of the runway as the taxiways.

This area was completely enclosed by a chain-link perimeter fence. Sections of the fence appeared to be capable of swinging open to permit aircraft access to the taxiways from hangars situated within the compound.

Perimeter towers set at compass points on the fence rose some thirty feet above the ground, and from these guard towers searchlight beacons swept the interior and exterior of the base.

Each security outpost was manned by a single guard and equipped with a pintle-mounted RPK 7.62 mm machine gun. Tallin had no doubt that together the guard posts could sweep the interior of the compound with a decimating crossfire.

Rows of low-rise barracks buildings stood at the leftmost section of the compound. A parade ground took up the main area of the base and beyond this, at the opposite end, was an enormous hangar, easily two hundred square feet in surface area, made of concrete with a corrugated steel roof.

Toward the west end of the base, Tallin could make out the C^{3}I installation, a low-rise cinder-block building without windows whose rooftop bristled with antennas and beside which were positioned banks of forward-staring phased radar arrays.

Tallin looked away from the binocular lenses for a moment and consulted his wrist chronometer. It was past 0516 hours by now and dawn was well on its way to breaking.

Piotr and Barsov flanked Tallin as he took one final look through the field glasses. He then put aside the binoculars with which he had been subjecting the base to a thorough scan, imprinting every detail on his memory.

"How long will it be safe to wait here?" Tallin asked Barsov.

The guide from the village thought for a minute before replying. "We can stay here for a few hours more. Then I would say we might be picked up by a patrol or spotted from the air, because there is fairly regular helicopter traffic in and out of this place."

"We'll wait a while," Tallin told the two men. "I want to try and see what kind of activity patterns develop for as long as possible."

In addition to this, Tallin wanted more on-site information pertaining to the weak points of the base. He would need to have these data in order to formulate a comprehensive plan of attack. This meant that he would ask for a volunteer to go inside in order to conduct a soft recce probe.

Tallin asked Barsov if he knew of an alternate route inside the base which could be used by a commando who wanted to scout the place out.

"As a matter of fact, I was just about to bring that same option up," the guide said with a slight smile. "One of the villagers who came up this way to look over the base discovered a drainage pipe large enough for a man to crawl through. It comes up inside the fence, about ten meters beyond. The villager was captured, but I myself have established that the route is still usable."

Barsov did not add that it was his younger brother Grigory who had been captured inside the base and had probably been summarily executed as a spy. He told Tallin that the mouth of the pipe lay about thirty feet to the north, across the ridgeline. Piotr volunteered at once to penetrate the base and have a look around.

Tallin waited until the sun had come up and the morning had fully broken. The lights in the guard towers had been long since extinguished when he decided that Piotr should go in.

Tallin sent Barsov to guide Piotr to the mouth of the pipe, instructing Piotr in those features which he wanted him to pay special attention to and report back on in intricate detail.

Less than fifteen minutes later, Barsov returned and reported that Piotr had gone into the drainage duct and was now on his way into the base. Barsov, Tallin and Gennady would wait at the site until Piotr's return.

The rest of the commando team would redeploy to the peasant village, farther down the slope of the mountain. When the entire unit had reassembled at the village, final plans for hitting the target would be firmed up. And then the strike would commence.

Piotr found the going relatively easy as he proceeded along a level path for approximately four hundred yards before coming to a circular shaftway, approximately three feet in circumference extending vertically, whose walls were made of brick and oozed moisture from their pointings.

Scaling the wall by means of a succession of rusted iron cleats projecting from it, Piotr climbed to the top of what was certainly a dry well.

Cautiously lifting the wooden cover a crack, he took a look around him and heard the crunch of boot soles against gravel a few moments later.

A greatcoated guard walking his perimeter passed just abreast of Piotr's concealed position. When the guard had finally gone by, Piotr climbed out of the dry well and moved stealthily toward the cover of the nearest building by his position.

One of the chief sites which Tallin had wanted Piotr to have a look at was the large aircraft hangar that he had spotted on his binocular scan of the base.

Piotr crept up to one of the hangar's small windows and peered inside. It was just as Tallin had believed it would be: there were two mammoth Blackjack bombers which were being worked on by ground crew mechanics in grease-stained overalls.

Technicians were at the same time loading an AS-15 nuclear cruise missile into the bomb bays of the heavy bombers. The ALCM was sleek and barracuda-shaped and it measured about a dozen feet long. The supersonic missile had small vertical stabilizers located at its rear and cone-shaped rocket nacelles for propulsion as well as two forward-mounted stub wings.

Piotr next moved stealthily to have a look at the base ammo dump and C³I center, getting as near to both of these well-guarded installations as was possible.

Twenty minutes had elapsed since his penetration of the base, and Piotr now decided that he had already pressed his luck. He was preparing to make his way back to the dry well by means of which he had entered the compound when he suddenly heard the rumble of heavy trucks coming from directly behind him.

Standing stock-still, Piotr flattened himself against the side of the blockhouse. From his position there he had a good view of the installation's main gate and saw two heavy transports enter the compound, whereupon the troops on board piled out.

But the next sights that Piotr saw proved to be truly startling, for a staff car bearing a Russian air force colonel also pulled up, and a man and a woman, both wearing flight suits, emerged from the vehicle, to be marched at rifle point by a squad of soldiers across the parade ground toward the base commander's headquarters.

The red, white and blue flag patches on the shoulders of their flight suits left no doubt in Piotr's mind as to the fact that these two prisoners were Americans.

Piotr received another shock when he saw the heavy-set form of the base commander exit the headquarters building and stand, in the uniform of a GRU general, awaiting the approach of the two prisoners with a cool, surveying glance.

Despite Piotr's not being able to have a close-up look at the commander's face, the man's cock-of-the-walk gait and his arrogant bearing identified him to the Afghan veteran as clearly as a set of fingerprints, and Piotr knew that this news would be as startling to Tallin as it was to him.

And then Piotr received his next, and final, surprise

as the main gate swung open again to admit a long flatbed truck with a tarp-covered cargo lashed to it by heavy ropes.

The camouflage-pattern tarp covered most of the truck's cargo, but it did not conceal the sleek nose of the black aircraft or the contoured edges of its double-delta wings.

It was a type of aircraft that Piotr had never seen before. A black aircraft without any sort of insignia. Piotr burned the image of the plane into his mind. Tallin would want to know every detail concerning it.

24

Cox watched the military man in the general's uniform who sat across the desk from him in the Spartanly appointed office.

Fyodor Aleksiev had a face which appeared to have been carved from a block of granite, its features chiseled with blunt, sharp strokes that had left clean, angular edges. His flinty gray eyes had the penetrating aspect of a hunting falcon and his head sat atop the bearlike frame of a man born with the natural power to command.

Aleksiev smiled tautly at his prisoners. In the months since setting his plans into motion, he had often wondered as to the sort of response that the blinding of the Americans' and his own country's reconsats would bring.

Because he had expected a full frontal attack by shock troops from the Center at the goading of their new capitalist masters, Aleksiev had strengthened perimeter defenses at the secret mountain stronghold.

He had never suspected that the Americans would instead field one of their superannuated spyplanes in an attempt to gather reconnaissance intelligence now unavailable to them in the wake of the destruction of their orbital satellite network.

At first, Aleksiev had marveled at the naïveté of the Americans in carrying out such a clumsy tactic and suspected that it was nothing more than a diversion from the true, hammerblow-style assault which was in the offing.

However, once he had taken the opportunity for a firsthand look at the SR-71 and had been shown by base technicians the new and ingenious ways ·in which the aircraft had been retrofitted for its current mission, Aleksiev's initial response had turned into one of respect and admiration.

The plane was a unique hybrid of past and present technologies and it had, on consideration, been the single available intelligence platform fit to undertake the mission.

The pilot of the spyplane was unique as well. Aleksiev had read with amusement the report turned in by the smarting air force captain Magadan, who had been outwitted by the American's stellar flying skills on several occasions.

"Congratulations," Aleksiev said to his prisoners in a heavy Russian accent, looking from Cox to Gilroy. "You have both performed the impossible. Not only have you succeeded in gathering intelligence on this base, but you have also eluded destruction by the finest pilots in the world."

He stood up, raising his tall, broad frame to its full six-foot height, and walked around to the front of his desk, where he perched on the edge.

"You may be wondering what will be happening to you next," Aleksiev went on, then proceeded to answer his own words. "You will be detained here, of course, and you will soon be interrogated. If you cooperate fully, I can assure you that there will be no problems. Are there any questions?"

"Now that you mention it, there are a couple," Cox said to the big, rawboned bear of a Russian general. "For openers, how do you expect to get away with blowing away half the human race? You don't actually believe you'll be able to pull it off, do you?"

Aleksiev chuckled and shook his head in exasperation. Here was further proof that Americans were as importunate a breed as they were rapacious. He would have seen to it that such disrespect from his own men would have brought grave punishment, but he would humor this bantam cock of a man. Indeed, on reflection, he decided there would be no harm in telling the American precisely what he intended to accomplish.

Doing so would bring the general pleasure.

"The Commonwealth of Independent States is in the process of disintegration," Aleksiev began. "I intend to save it from this inevitable decay, a cancerous growth of the same sort that has taken root in your own blighted country. But in order to save the patient, I fear we shall have to surgically remove some parts of the body politic.

"This is just what I intend to do. By subjecting your homeland to a nuclear attack, I will cause nuclear escalation to the point where the breakaway Russian republics are once again forced to reunify in the name of common cause."

"You're crazy, buster," Gilroy said to the general.

"Hardly," Aleksiev calmly replied, shaking his head as if lecturing small children who were far too naive to understand the higher principles he served. "It is you Americans who are insane. You and your demented culture that would sweep away all barriers, eradicate all distinctions between right and wrong, reduce everything to a hazy nothingness in the name of a democracy which has never truly been practiced.

"You talk of 'the failed experiment of Communism'? Look at what the equally failed experiment in so-called 'democracy' has meant to your own country—a complete breakdown in values, a rejection of even the more basic moral precepts. The same will not occur here in Russia. I will see to it."

The general would not be stopped. Cox and Gilroy saw the light of fanaticism shine in his eyes as he lectured them for the better part of an hour on his twisted messianic goals.

Communism was the salvation of mankind, he patently insisted.

Armed with its unifying vision, Marx and Lenin had taken a backward, near-feudal society and raised it from servitude to corrupt czars into a nation of workers, scientists and builders. Marxist-Lenin ideology was still sound, and a world in which Communism was no longer a vital force was a world that was better off reduced to nuclear embers.

Aleksiev was not alone in this view; many others shared his deeply felt conviction. His fanaticism had infected hundreds of fellow travelers and former Party apparatchiks who were still loyal to the old regime, who still clung to the cherished hope that they might be able to turn back the clock and make the phoenix of Communism rise from the ashes of its own self-inflicted decay.

As Cox listened to the general's diatribe, he realized that the voice was an old one, echoing into the present from decades gone by. It was a voice shared by Hitler, Mussolini and Josef Stalin.

It was a voice which preached the totalitarian rule of absolute law as an antidote to the fear of incipient anarchy and which claimed that each individual was unable to be held accountable for his or her own actions.

It was a voice which claimed that brute force and total, iron-fisted control were the only answers to the age-old question of how to make society run with a clockwork precision in which all men were cogs in a vast, smoothly turning wheel.

"You will now be taken to cells in the base stockade," Aleksiev concluded tersely. "You will have mess and then you will be briefed separately."

The general next called to his aide, who saluted Aleksiev and then led the two prisoners away at the point of an AKM assault rifle.

From their seats in the commander's office, Cox and Gilroy were marched back across the parade ground toward the base stockade. In the process, Cox scanned the installation, his trained eyes missing nothing as he built up a mental map of the large aircraft hangar and the Blackjack bombers parked therein.

If he succeeded in escaping, then knowing his way around would be of vital importance.

The Blackjack was in itself not the surest delivery system for nuclear weapons, but with long-range cruise missile capability, its kill potential from a position of standoff engagement was awesome. The Blackjack could launch its complement of nuclear-tipped ALCMs from a location far from the continental United States.

The AS-15 air-launched cruise missiles were relatively slow, but their terrain-hugging, depressed-trajectory flight paths, which brought them to their targets below the threshold of radar detection systems, made them hard to kill; and the one-megaton punches they packed made them highly effective even against time-urgent hard targets such as missile silos.

Mad as a hatter though the general might be, his tactical reasoning was nevertheless as sound as a bell.

Even a single strike from a one-megaton cruise missile, producing a blast ten to twenty times the size of the Hiroshima bomb, would immediately set into motion a pattern of upward-spiraling nuclear escalation that would almost certainly result in the redivision of the East and the West into heavily armed camps.

But the terminal logic of the general was faulty in at

least one critical respect: the nuclear endgame that he contemplated would not see the rebirth of the Communist state.

Instead it would lay a death trap for humanity as reciprocal reprisals set in motion an automatic chain of kill and counterkill that would not cease until the earth was sterilized of every last living bacterium.

Soon Cox and Gilroy were marched into the receiving area of the building which housed the base stockade. Cox was surprised to find that their flight suits, complete with helmets as well as the P-90 CAWs they had been issued as personal-defense weapons, were lying out in the open on a trestle table in the crotch of one of the olive-drab painted walls.

A stocky Russian sergeant major, wearing jackboots which cracked sharply on the wood planking of the stockade's floor, drew his gun, a 9 mm Makarov automatic pistol.

Hectoring them in coarse street Russian and gesturing threateningly with the Makarov, he was able to communicate to his American prisoners to walk through a steel door and into a corridor lined on either side with iron-barred holding pens.

With the Makarov trained on Cox, the sergeant major used a key to open one of the cells and gestured for Gilroy to go inside. Cox was locked in the cell adjacent to Gilroy's.

Like hers, the pen he was in was roughly ten feet by twelve feet in size, with bars at one end that looked out onto a bare cinder-block-walled corridor and a small window positioned high on the rear wall, which was also barred.

Holstering his pistol, the sergeant major said something to Gilroy and licked his lips, then spoke to Cox as well, apparently laughing at a joke he'd made. They heard the stomping of his jackboots on the plank floor of the corridor, followed by the grating of the heavy door hinges before the final thud of the door slamming shut.

"What do you think he said?" Gilroy asked Cox.

"I don't know," Cox replied, lying down on the rough metal plank that was bolted at hip level to the cell wall. "But whatever it was, he sure thought it was funny."

The interior of the drainage pipe echoed softly with the clatter of Piotr's stealthy progress toward its mouth.

As he trod through the murk of the pipe on a half crouch, the vasaltnicki kept his SITES Spectre SMG at the ready for instant deployment. Light soon glimmered faintly at the other end of the large pipe, and Piotr reached the point at which he'd entered a few minutes later.

Tallin and Barsov were waiting below the place where the mouth of the pipe projected from near the top of an earthen embankment, the muzzles of their weapons pointing at the man who was now emerging from the mouth of the drainage pipe.

Recognizing Piotr, they put their guns away and helped him climb down the embankment from the mouth of the pipe.

"Chief," he said to Tallin, a little out of breath from his exertions, "I've seen some pretty amazing things. For one, they've got two American fliers held prisoner on the base. These two were apparently captured in some sort of aircraft which I think I can try to sketch for you."

"That is certainly interesting news, Piotr," Tallin told his friend after listening carefully to his brief. "And we will have to take these new developments into account in our planning for the raid."

Piotr held up his hand. "Wait. There's more," he

went on. "And it's the most unbelievable part of all. Do you know who is the commander of this installation?" he asked. "It's Aleksiev!"

"General Fyodor Aleksiev?" Tallin said, a look of amazement spreading across his face.

"Yes, one and the same," Piotr assured the team's commander with a nod as he sipped from his canteen and wiped away the sweat which had collected on his brow. "I thought you would be interested to hear this piece of news. You more than anyone else in all of Russia owe that bastard a payback."

"And now I have been granted my chance," Tallin affirmed, clenching his fist until the knuckles whitened with tension as his cold gray eyes took on a faraway look and his mind turned back to the rugged mountain country of the Afghanistani south and the base treachery of over a decade past.

"Come. Let's get back to the village. We have a great deal of planning to do," Tallin said after a moment. With Barsov in the lead, the three of them began moving down the side of the mountain toward the peasant village below.

25

Their faces cammied in irregular stripes of non-reflective black and green, the vasaltnicki commandos reached their rally point on the heights overlooking the clandestine base. Here they would rest for a short while and receive their final briefing after Tallin took the time to make a last recce of the area.

Night-seeing field glasses held up to his eyes, Tallin carefully and diligently scouted out the base below. After a few minutes of long-range scanning, he determined that little in the way of new patterns of movement had emerged since his last surveillance of the strike perimeter.

The plan of attack that the commando had formulated called for three things to happen in rapid succession in order for it to be successfully carried out.

First, the compound would have to be breached.

Second, the C³I blockhouse and the ground radars which it supported would have to be neutralized in order to knock out communication with troops or aircraft outside the base.

Finally and most importantly, the Blackjack bombers and their complement of eight AS-15 nuclear cruise missiles would need to be destroyed on the ground.

If his team was able to carry out these three main mission objectives, then General Aleksiev's personal fate would be immaterial, a mere loose end to be tied up later. Stripped of the trappings of his power, he would be reduced to a hunted man whose ultimate fate would be assured.

Still and all, a priority for Tallin would be to deliver the final kick to the seat of the treacherous general's pants.

Tallin had a purely personal score to settle with the man whose physical appearance was the embodiment of the Russian bear and whom his countrymen looked up to as a hero. It was a grudge that dated back over a decade, to a hamlet in the battle-torn mountain country of Afghanistan.

The diamond flame of anger spurred by the outrage which Aleksiev had inflicted on the then-Spetsnaz colonel Boris Tallin still burned hot inside the commando, and Tallin hoped he would get the chance to quench the heat inside him by means of direct action.

More than for himself and for those of his men who shared his anger with him, Tallin sought retribution for others who were not with him today: the brave comrades whose bones rotted in the desolate hills of Afghanistan because of the actions of the man who had once led them.

While Tallin conducted his final recce of the base, thoughts of an entirely different sort were going through the mind of the sergeant major who was in charge of the stockade.

The American woman flier interested him.

He found her attractive, quite apart from the fact that she was the only woman he had laid eyes on in months—unless, of course, one counted the hags in the village below, which he emphatically did not. The sergeant major was horny, but he was not blind.

The sergeant major had come into the block of holding cells several times and spoken to her in the coarse

Russian of the St. Petersburg streets, telling Gilroy things he would not have uttered had he believed that she possessed the ability to understand what he was saying.

He came in again for another visit, late in the night. This time he received the shock of his life.

The American woman bared her large, round breasts as she leaned against the cell's rear wall, coyly sucking her index finger. The sergeant major licked his lips and noted that the male American pilot was sound asleep on his bunk in the adjacent holding pen.

The woman flier took her finger from her mouth and brought it to her lips in a signal for the jailer to come into her cell quietly.

The Russian nodded in an understanding that transcended all languages. His cock now hard, the sergeant major could not resist such an invitation, despite the warnings of his own common sense.

Throwing the cell door open, he strode inside, already tugging at the zipper of his trousers to free the erect organ that was confined within. Gilroy signified to him by hand gestures that she wanted to perform fellatio on him, and as he stood awaiting his reward for diligence, with his cock sticking out, she knelt in front of him, as though preparing to commence the act.

But a moment later, instead of giving the sergeant major what he expected, Gilroy had shoved the beefy Russian against the bars of the cell, using all of her strength.

Cox was behind the struggling jailer now, his hand across the sergeant major's mouth while Gilroy delivered a solid toe kick to his exposed testicles.

The Russian groaned against Cox's hand and slid down to the hard concrete of the cell, whimpering like a beaten cur.

Gilroy was out in the corridor a few seconds later. In possession of the cellblock master key, Cox was soon also released.

Together they made tracks into the outer office beyond the block of stockade pens. Their flight suits were still lying atop the trestle table, just as they had been when the fliers had been taken into the stockade hours before.

A further search of the quarters turned up two large duffle bags into which the flight suits and helmets had been stuffed, as well as handcuffs and adhesive tape with which to secure the sergeant major, whom Cox locked inside Gilroy's cell after making certain that he was immobilized.

"We've got company," Cox heard Gilroy call out as he was coming back to the stockade's front area. "An officer and a foot soldier with an AKM. Looks like . . . yeah, they're heading for us."

Cox joined her at the corner of the window frame and confirmed her sighting. He gestured for Gilroy to flatten herself against the side of the door.

The interrogator and his escort did not know what had gone down inside the base stockade. They would not be expecting the prisoners to have escaped, but instead to find them waiting inside their cells, cowed and psychologically receptive to their interrogation techniques.

As soon as the second soldier with the rifle was inside the room, Cox smashed him across the base of the skull with a heavy iron ashtray he'd taken from the olive-drab metal desk that stood up front. The soldier went down in a groaning, blood-spraying heap as the psychological-operations officer struggled to free the Makarov from the confines of its regulation holster.

A short burst of 5.70 mm high-velocity rounds from the whisper-quiet P-90 catapulted the officer across the desk, and he slid to the floorboards with his arms outflung.

"Any indication we've been made?" asked Cox of Gilroy as he pulled the officer and the enlisted man out of sight behind the desk.

"Negative, boss," Gilroy told him at once.

"Good. Now climb into the soldier's uniform. Don't worry about the fit. I'll go out and get the staff car they drove up to the stockade in and you'll get inside quickly. It's dark, so if you move fast, we may be able to get away with the deception."

"It'll never work, boss," Gilroy said to Cox as she changed into her flight suit and put on the unconscious soldier's camo fatigues over the lightweight pressure suit.

"Remind me to tell you that you're the most negative person I've ever met," Cox returned. "Now jump to it. That's an order, Lieutenant."

"Aye, aye, sir," she responded mockingly. "Anything you say."

Cox was out the door a moment later and Gilroy heard the motor of the staff car start up as she finished donning the fatigues of the enlisted man, who was still out cold on the floor behind the desk.

Cox brought the staff car around to the front of the stockade building and Gilroy climbed in after dumping the duffle bags containing their flight helmets into the vehicle's backseat.

All at once the sound of thunder boomed and echoed through the still night air as the black sky lit up with gouts of fire and cascades of sparks. Taken aback, Cox realized that a series of powerful explosions had just rocked the base.

"What's happening?" Gilroy asked Cox.

"The base is being hit," Cox returned as heaven and earth convulsed around them. "I think we're under attack!"

26

The vasaltnickis hit the perimeter of the base with multiply launched RPG-18 HEAT rockets. The first burst of high-explosive and armor-piercing shrapnel knocked out the guards in the security towers, blowing the four crow's nests to smithereens amid a spray of hot yellow sparks.

As the main element of the commando assault unit raced in a spearhead formation into the base compound, two squads deployed from the flanks of the cutting edge of the triangle.

The mission assigned these two squads was to take out the C^3I installation and the hangar containing the Blackjack bombers and their nuclear cruise missiles.

The main strike force element with Tallin on point set up the man-portable RPG-18 multiple rocket launchers in front of the barracks buildings. The manpad's high-explosive rounds slammed into the wooden structures, blowing them to flinders and killing most of the troops who were billeted inside.

Those few survivors staggered out into the night and were suddenly mowed down by squad machine gunners who had set up with the unit's Ultimax 100 automatic weapons. By this means, resistance was decimated and the enemy personnel whom the vasaltnickis had to contend with quickly cut down to a manageable force level.

While Squad A was dealing with the base troops, the

two other assault squads were already taking out their assigned mission objectives.

Squad B, headed by Gennady, blew the door of the C³I building inward with a HEAT rocket burst. Standing on either side of the vacant doorway, Gennady then pitched a flash-bang grenade into the interior.

Stunned by the loud reports and strobing flashes, personnel within the blockhouse were completely disoriented. Eyes goggled and ears plugged, Gennady and the three other squad members came in with their SITES Spectres spraying sustained bursts of PB ammunition at the personnel, the compact SMGs taking them down quickly with accurately vectored fire.

"Damn," Gennady cursed as he looked around the bullet-pocked command and control center. He had noticed that one of the computer screens bore a flashing message, the Cyrillic characters indicating that a preprogrammed distress code had been keystroked into the unit only moments prior to the lightning attack.

Apparently one of the C³I operators had managed to get off the code before he was taken out.

The strike team wasted no time in planting time-fuzed submunitions inside the C³I unit.

Setting the LCD readouts for a three-minute detonation delay, Gennady and his crew made tracks from the building and dived for the cover of some heavy vehicles parked nearby, just as the blockhouse blew up with a thunderous roar and a balloon of incinerating flame reared skyward on a pillar of fire.

Squad C had by this time reached the hangar and encountered armed resistance from sentries posted there. Some members of the subunit were wounded in the brief though violent fight to take the fortified position. However, within minutes after storming the hangar, Mikhail's squad was inside and had secured the area.

While two members of the unit set up with Ultimax

5.56 mm light machine guns and stood guard, the rest of the squad was already unshipping the shaped prismatic charges and slotting them throughout the hangar.

The prismatic shape of the charge would channel the blast effect produced by the detonating plastic explosive into a compressed and amplified shock wave which was capable of generating tremendous destructive force.

Having been assigned its tasks and drilled by Tallin throughout the planning session of the previous night, the squad went quickly about its rehearsed procedures, and within five minutes of elapsed mission time, had completed slotting the charges throughout the hangar area in a phased array.

Because of the number of individual submunitions that had been planted throughout the hangar area, these charges were not individually timed. Instead they were hot-linked to a remote control panel which could trigger their phased detonations from a safe distance.

"We're finished here," the demo crew leader said to Mikhail after the final charges were slotted into place by the team.

"Good. Let's go," Mikhail told him.

Moments later, the hangar demolition detail was hightailing it across the parade ground. Mikhail ordered his squad to flatten out as he too lay prone and triggered the first main control button of the three phased tiers of hot-linked demolition charges.

The primary charges detonated immediately. Then the secondaries and tertiaries went, their combined blast effect producing an explosion of such intensity that it created an instant fire storm.

At the epicenter of the burnout zone, temperatures in excess of one thousand degrees Celsius were reached and exceeded within seconds.

These high-magnitude temperatures were sufficiently hot to melt and fuse all metal components of both the aircraft and its payload of nuclear missiles except those such as engine air intakes, which were constructed of titanium alloy. These would not melt under even such extreme temperatures.

Because bringing a radioactive isotope to the critical mass necessary to produce nuclear explosions required a precisely controlled sequence of events, there was no danger of the nukes detonating from the effects of the explosions.

Across the compound, Tallin and Piotr saw the hangar blow sky-high in a massive explosion which caused it to disintegrate into an incandescent gas cloud of fast-rising flame.

"They've done it!" Tallin shouted above the clamor of war, which dinned and echoed off the surrounding mountainsides like rolling thunder.

Now there remained final priorities to be attended to.

For Tallin, there was a personal score to settle if he was able to track down the general. But first his task would be to find the two Americans if he could and assist them in escape, if that were possible.

As Cox and Gilroy were standing beside the commandeered staff car, hearing the blast of the sudden explosions which had rocked the base and wondering what was happening, they saw Tallin along with Piotr and his squad race toward them.

As soon as Tallin made visual contact he called out, "Friend," in English and reached the Americans, who were training weapons of an advanced configuration on him which Piotr had never before seen.

"Who are you?" asked Cox, steadying the P-90 on the Russian assault-team leader.

"I command this unit," Tallin told him in thickly accented English. "We have instructions to destroy this base and to help you escape."

"Orders?" Cox asked. "From who exactly?"

"From the highest levels." Tallin went on cryptically. "As your own orders undoubtedly come. That is all I can say. We want you to return to your side and deliver a message. Make certain your superiors understand that we Russians have cleaned up our own mess. My men will see you to your aircraft and enable you to fly it out of here."

"Are you out of your mind?" Cox asked the Russian. "Fly it out? No way, pal. Running an instrument check alone will take more time than—"

"There *isn't* time to argue!" Tallin cut in abruptly. "And I'm afraid your chances would not be very good if you remained with us. We are—how do you Americans say?—expendable. And without you letting your people know about what really happened here, the world may still be plunged into a nuclear war which will destroy us all."

Cox knew then that the Russian commando was right.

There was no other solution to their dilemma except to dare the impossible and fly the Blackbird out of the base in a last-ditch run to get back to the Watchtower mission-support facility on Svalbard Island.

"Make your decision," Tallin pressed them. "Time is running out quickly."

"Okay," Cox returned after a long beat as the staccato reports of an exchange of automatic fire were heard in the distance. "Let's do it."

The Russian's words had convinced him. Flying out of the area might be suicidal, but so was remaining in these mountains with the extracting commando team. Cox and Gilroy were caught between the rock and the hard place, and it made little difference which course they chose.

Tallin gestured at the big man in camo fatigues

standing to his right. "Piotr will take you to the plane. *Dah svidahnya.*"

Saying that, Tallin turned and sprinted off toward the parade ground, soon disappearing into the chaotic jumble of figures running through the darkness amid the sporadic bursts of explosions and the sudden flashes of automatic-weapons fire.

"Where's he going?" Cox asked.

"He has personal business to settle," Piotr responded. "But we must go now."

Stripping off their commandeered uniforms to expose their lightweight flight suits worn underneath, Cox and Gilroy jumped into the staff car.

As they removed their helmets from the duffle bags containing them, Piotr got behind the wheel and the staff car peeled away from the stockade building with a banshee screech of smoking rubber.

27

It was all over but the shouting; the general saw this all too clearly.

His grand strategy was going the way of the gouts of flame which gushed skyward, fading with the echoes of the explosions which consumed the aircraft hangar along with the rest of the structures in the compound.

Removing his uniform, Aleksiev donned unmarked camouflage fatigues and loaded a clip of 9 mm rounds into a Wz63 RAK machine pistol, which he slid into a black leather pit holster slung across his barrel chest.

There might yet be a means of escape left open to him. Aleksiev still enjoyed tremendous popularity throughout the Russian Republic, and he had taken great pains to ensure that secrecy concerning the clandestine base was total.

If that glorified apparatchik Pavlovich dared to challenge him in public, Aleksiev would come out the better man, of this he felt certain. The Russian President was a man who was walking on thin ice as it was.

No, the general realized, Pavlovich would keep his silence, if for no other reason than to save his own worthless neck.

There were still millions in hard currency on deposit in numbered bank accounts in Switzerland, the Caymans and elsewhere. Even in the unlikely event that matters deteriorated to the point where his life was in jeopardy, Aleksiev could still retire to a comfortable exile where he might yet find a way to return to the Motherland in triumph.

A leader's first duty was to survive at any and all costs, Aleksiev believed. He had put this maxim into practice before and had become expert in doing so. Now as then, the general had made certain that an emergency escape corridor was available to him as a safety measure.

Such measures had saved his life on at least one other occasion, during the surprise attack by Afghani Mujahideen on the Spetsnaz-fortified position in the Khogiania district of Nangarhar Province.

On that occasion it had been a helicopter rather than a tunnel that had shuttled him to safety, along with a fortune in gold bullion which he had stolen from the coffers of the provincial capital.

Later he had learned that only Spetsnaz Colonel Tallin and a handful of his men had survived the attack. The colonel had attempted to have Aleksiev brought up on charges of cowardice under fire, but he had quashed this attempt and had made certain, years later, that Tallin was placed in Lefortovo, where he would not again threaten him.

And now the trapdoor concealed beneath the rug in his office would lead Aleksiev to a tunnel which had been excavated beneath the parade ground of the installation.

The escape tunnel stretched several hundred yards beneath the hard-packed surface of earth and clay and terminated in the dense pine woods beyond the camp.

There was a cave there, its mouth well concealed, in which part of his cache of Kabul gold, weapons and a vehicle had been secreted against precisely this eventuality. Loading a musette bag with false identity papers and a few thousand in hard currency, which he had prepared for this contingency arising, Aleksiev moved quickly, knowing that delay could well prove fatal.

Tallin reached the commander's office moments before the general could make good his escape. The vasaltnicki leader saw the upraised wooden cover of the trapdoor and Aleksiev preparing to step down into it and descend the ladder which led to the tunnel floor.

"Aleksiev!" Tallin shouted. "Don't move, you sonofabitch!"

The general stopped in mid-stride.

He had heard a voice from the past, a voice it was impossible for him to be hearing. Yet a glance in the direction of the voice told Aleksiev that it was indeed Tallin who had shouted, and a cold dread gripped him.

Tallin fired the Spectre SMG in his hand, spraying a burst of parabellum bullets across the office which shattered glass and thudded into the wooden walls. With only his upper torso visible above the floor, Aleksiev returned fire, using the RAK machine pistol, forcing Tallin to tuck back around the frame of the office doorway.

In a heartbeat Aleksiev had dropped down into the guts of the tunnel. On a flat-out run Tallin followed, catching sight of the running man about thirty yards ahead of him.

"Stop, damn you!" Tallin shouted as he raised the Spectre to shoulder-fire position with its wire buttstock retracted and propped against his armpit for stabilized fire in single-shot mode.

The brattling of the Wz63 came in answer as Aleksiev snapped a burst over his shoulder.

Hastily delivered, the wildfire burst was inaccurate, but it succeeded in forcing Tallin to flatten against the tunnel wall as bullets whined past his position, and the stray rounds buried themselves harmlessly into the earthen walls of the subterranean passage.

By the time Tallin had regained his footing and was in place for a clear shot at his quarry, Aleksiev was already out of sight around a dogleg bend in the tunnel. With a shouted oath, Tallin broke into another flat-out run, the Spectre clutched in his hand and back on full-auto fire select.

He found Aleksiev waiting for him in ambush around the other side of the bend. Flattened against the wall, the general had leapt from cover and now trained the Wz63 at Tallin's midsection.

"We meet again at last, Boris Mikhail'ch," Aleksiev said to Tallin, who had pulled up to a dead stop. "It has been several years since we served the Motherland together. You look well."

"And you are stained with blood," Tallin said to the general. "You slaughtered my men. You took loyal, brave Spetsnaz and killed them like dogs in pursuit of your lust for the gold of Kabul, and then you left them to die in the dust."

"I did what I had to do," Aleksiev told Tallin with a shrug. "As we all must. Now you will slowly place your weapon on the ground and kick it away from you. Good," he continued a moment later. "Now proceed down the tunnel." He gestured with the muzzle of the small, deadly SMG in his fist. "I will have need of strong hands to help load some equipment aboard my vehicle."

Stripped of the Spectre SMG, Tallin marched ahead of the general, who pressed him forward down the tunnel at a brisk pace.

They reached the end of the tunnel minutes later, and Aleksiev pushed aside a heavy steel door which gave access into the interior of a mountain cave complete with stalactites and stalagmites.

A few feet on, Aleksiev pulled a small flashlight from his pocket and shone its beam around until he had located a powerful battery-operated torch, which he turned on. It gave enough light to illuminate the cavern and Tallin saw a Volga all-terrain vehicle parked near a stack of wooden shipping crates.

"Those crates on the floor. Load them in back," Aleksiev said to Tallin, gesturing at the pile of wooden boxes against one of the cave walls.

Tallin proceeded to load the boxes on board the truck, under Aleksiev's watchful eye. "You're doing fine, Tallin," Aleksiev commented mockingly. "You were always a strong—"

Tallin had wheeled around and heaved a crate toward the speaker, striking a glancing blow on Aleksiev's gun hand. The machine pistol went off, sending a burst of ricocheting 9 mm rounds into the black rock face of the cavern wall, but the weapon still remained clutched in the general's hands.

Tallin grabbed hold of the big man's wrist, but Aleksiev was as strong as he was determined to retain his weapon, and the vicelike fingers did not let go of the RAK, even after repeated smashings of his hand against the rock wall.

Determined to finish the fight, Tallin rammed his knee into Aleksiev's groin and the general sank into a half crouch, gasping in pain as the machine pistol dropped from his numb fingers and clattered to the floor. Tallin followed through with a spinning side kick to the general's face which missed its mark as the general rolled aside at the final instant before the foot blow connected.

Aleksiev launched himself forward, bellowing in anger like the wounded bear he resembled, ignoring the searing pain in his crippled hand and wounded groin.

The impact of collision with the general's massive

bulk sent Tallin windmilling backward against the steel bumper of the Volga ATV, and Aleksiev pressed home his attack, hitting his adversary in the face with several pile-driving, haymaker-style blows, then picked up a large stone and, lifting it high above him, prepared to smash it down on the head of his punch-drunk adversary.

Recovering his wits in a surge of adrenaline, Tallin dodged the death blow and responded with a forearm smash to the side of Aleksiev's throat as the small boulder clanged against the chassis of the all-terrain vehicle. The arm blow sent the general reeling sideways, gagging as he struggled to regain his breath.

Staggering like a drunken man as the cave swam before his eyes, his face turned a bright red, Aleksiev suddenly caught the dull gleam of the Wz63 machine pistol, which had been knocked from his hand when Tallin had first attacked him.

The general dived for the machine pistol, but before he could bring it up to fire, Tallin, who also had seen the RAK and knew what Aleksiev intended, slid out the coffin-handled knife scabbarded at his boot top and pitched it underhand with great power and expert aim. The razor-sharp six-inch blade struck its target with perfect precision. Burrowing into Aleksiev's heart, it penetrated to the steel cross guard.

Aleksiev dropped the weapon he had just picked up and tried to pull the knife from the blood-jetting wound on his upper left torso. Bubbles of bright blood escaped from his lips as his eyes rolled up in his head, and he keeled sideways before crumpling to the cavern floor in a floundering heap and then, finally, went completely still.

Tallin used a crowbar from the Volga to break open the packing crates and inspect their contents. As he pried away the slats of wood, he saw the gleam of bars of solid gold, each bearing the inscription of the Bank of Kabul.

There were millions here, Tallin realized: millions which rightfully belonged to the dead Spetsnaz whose remains lay forgotten in the desolate hill country of Afghanistan.

28

Piotr brought the staff car to a screeching halt beside the grounded Blackbird.

At once his men jumped out, and while Piotr stood guard with his Ultimax 100 LMG, the vasaltnickis rushed to the immobilized spyplane and stripped off the camouflage tarp that covered its fuselage, leaving the SR-71 still hitched to the tow bar by which it was connected to the tractor.

The entire base was still gripped in the convulsive upheavals of the strike, and enemy stragglers could still be expected to be encountered in the vicinity, although Mikhail's and Gennady's teams had reported via communications transceiver that the opposition was crushed and that prisoners were being rounded up.

Climbing atop the cab of the Russian military vehicle, Cox assisted Gilroy in clambering into the SR's cockpit, then followed himself.

With the cockpit's front and rear hatches still retracted back on their hinges, Cox and Gilroy immediately activated the SR-71's flight systems, encouraged to find that all the chiclets read green consistently.

The single critical factor was the extent of the fuel reserves remaining in the SR-71's tanks.

The level of fuel was down to less than half of the plane's twenty-thousand-gallon capacity, and Cox began using the on-board flight computer to determine whether or not the fuel supply would be sufficient to get them to where they needed to go.

The level of fuel was a critical factor.

He and Gilroy would have to fly out on the remaining reserves or continue to be grounded. Even if an alternate supply source of JP-7 were available, the specialized high-temperature sealants which kept the fuel inside the aircraft during flight operations would not be available.

Minutes after running his preflight systems check, Cox heaved himself out of the cockpit and climbed back down to the ground. He then began attacking the underbelly of the aircraft with a torque wrench taken from an emergency repair kit housed in a cockpit gear compartment.

"What the hell are you doing?" Piotr asked the American in surprise as he watched Cox go to work.

"Getting rid of excess weight," Cox responded, shouting back to the Russian. "With fuel critical, every excess pound will count in getting this bird back into the air, let alone back to our base."

Piotr now looked up to see that Gilroy was throwing out of the cockpit electronics modules she'd unfastened from their mounting racks, which then went crashing to the tarmac.

Using every precious minute they could spare, Cox and Gilroy stripped the Blackbird of as much dead weight as they were able to remove from the aircraft.

The SR's multimillion-dollar surveillance cameras and other reconnaissance gear had been vital to the mission prior to their being forced down in Russian territory but were now worse than useless.

Its extra weight penalty might wind up costing them their lives, and Cox and Gilroy worked feverishly to strip the plane of every last ounce of noncritical hardware.

Back in the cockpit, Cox was running through his preflight systems check while Piotr's vasaltnickis were firing up the engine of the tractor that the SR was hitched to, hot-wiring the vehicle's electrical system and starting the motor, which ratcheted for a moment, then came suddenly to life with a powerful roar.

"Look alive!" Piotr suddenly shouted to his commandos, spotting a group of stragglers coming up on their position at three o'clock clutching Kalashnikov auto-rifles.

Within moments the stuttering bolt clatter of automatic weapons rent the air as tracer rounds sent red-and-green bolts streaking through the night in a lethal crisscross between the vasaltnickis and the squad of armed base personnel.

Piotr counted four men in the enemy squad.

Ordinary ground troops, they did not pose an insurmountable threat, but he was also aware that the longer they were pinned down in this position, the greater the odds were that reinforcements would arrive or that, worse yet, the Blackbird would be damaged in the firefight and unable to take off.

All that would have to happen in order to turn the Blackbird into a fireball would be a single tracer round striking its fuselage in the right spot.

Tallin had explained that the plane was, in effect, a huge fuel bladder, and a single stray bullet could ignite the high-octane aviation fuel that the plane carried in a microinstant.

Seeing one of the squad members breaking from his position while his comrades threw up covering fire, Piotr rough-spotted the Ultimax through its metal sights, tracked ahead of the running figure and squeezed off a tumbling burst of 5.56 mm bullets.

The mobile figure instantly came to a halt and the running soldier's feet lost all semblance of coordina-

tion. He promptly fell in a sprawling heap and lay un-
moving on the bloodstained ground.

Pulling two mini-grenades which had been secured to
chest webbing by their cotter pins, Piotr called to his
men for covering fire. In a pulsebeat, the three remaining troopers tucked down their heads to avoid being hit
by the wall of lead thrown up by the former Spetsnaz.

Piotr was already up, pitching the grenades high to
initiate an airburst effect.

The toss was precisely timed and the grenades exploded over the heads of the soldiers just as they were
whipping their AK-47s up again to return a volley of
answering fire.

Hundreds of razor-sharp metal splinters spraying out
in a thirty-foot blast radius were driven into the flesh of
the three soldiers, killing them instantly as the submunitions went off.

"Igor, Grigory! Are you ready?" Piotr shouted to his
men.

They hollered back that they were. Hearing this,
Piotr raced toward the front of the black, needle-nosed
American spyplane and called up to Cox, "Do you
think you can get her airborne?"

"It'll be dicey, but yes, I think I can," Cox shouted
down to Piotr, having established that his fuel reserves
would be sufficient to bring the Blackbird back to the
island in Norwegian territory within a reasonable factor
of safety.

"Then start your engines," Piotr told him. "We'll tow
you onto the runway now. Good luck!"

Piotr ran back to the staff car and threw the idling
vehicle into gear, screaming toward the large gate,
which, when swung open, provided access from the
hangar to one of the taxiways leading to the level
blacktop runway which had been specially constructed
to facilitate the landing and takeoff of heavy bombers

and should certainly be sufficient to permit the same for the SR-71.

Cox started the port and starboard Pratt & Whitney turbo ramjet engines, which flamed to life immediately, and kept them locked on the lowest level of thrust and dogged down the cockpit bubble as the truck wheeled the nose of the Blackbird around to point it toward the gate, which Piotr had now swung open.

Within minutes, the SR-71 was rolling through the gate on its three cast-titanium landing gear and onto the tarmac, with Piotr and one of his men riding shotgun in the staff car at their head.

Progress seemed agonizingly slow to Cox, who wished he were already airborne and in control of the plane, not trusting his fate to the hands of others, regardless of how capable they seemed.

Piotr stopped the staff car and held up his hand to signal to his man driving the tow tractor to stop as well. The driver promptly jumped onto the tarmac and un-hitched the American spyplane from its coupling.

Moments later, he had driven the tractor to the side of the runway and rejoined Piotr and Grigory in the staff car.

Cox saw Piotr flash him the thumbs-up signal and he returned the universal sign of encouragement as he throttled up the SR, hearing the Blackbird's powerful engines roar to life as the jet turbines spat flame into the night.

Soon Piotr and his vasaltnickis saw the Blackbird begin rolling forward under its own steam, gathering speed as its landing gear moved across the blacktop and its exhaust nacelles lit up the darkened terrain with scorching fire.

"Damn!" Piotr suddenly shouted.

From the head of the runway, barreling down on them now, was an armored personnel carrier.

In a few seconds, a .50-caliber machine gun mounted atop the APC began chattering away, steel-jacketed rounds thudding into the blacktop near the staff car and the fast-moving American plane.

Gunning the staff car's engine, Piotr shot the four-wheel-drive vehicle ahead of the accelerating plane while Igor, up top with the RPK machine gun, began cranking out 7.62 mm tracer rounds, which shot green streaks through the night, crisscrossing with the fire coming from the onrushing APC.

Now the staff car had driven well past the nose of the Blackbird and was closing fast with the slower and less maneuverable armored personnel carrier.

Grigory was already getting into position with the team's manpads system, hoisting the shoulder-fire-capable RPG-18 rocket launcher into position and acquiring the APC in its pop-up sighting reticle.

Triggering the first of the four armor-piercing rockets that the RPG fired, Grigory sent the first HEAT round arcing through the darkness on a trajectory that rammed it into the front glacis of the armored vehicle.

The warhead burst on impact, its explosive charge deforming a hollow conical metal chamber positioned in front of it to send a lethal needle of semi-molten shrapnel jetting into the petaled aperture it had torn in the armored hide of the APC.

Vortexing blast effect ruptured the lungs of the driver and the two other soldiers stationed inside the plate-steel-clad war wagon as burning metal dismembered limbs and ripped living bodies asunder.

The APC's top gunner was still firing, though, but a second rocket round promptly settled his hash. Now on fire, the APC slid off the earth embankment on the side of the blacktop runway and juddered to a halt as flames and dense black smoke shot from its burning interior.

By this time, Cox was midway along the runway and

applying maximum thrust as his landing gear lifted off the smooth asphalt surface and the Blackbird got airborne.

With the APC having been taken out, Piotr and his men jumped from the staff car and watched the sleek black spy craft turn her belly toward the sky as, with a deafening roar, the SR-71 streaked up into the inky blackness of the night.

Moments later, the spyplane had disappeared entirely from view over the line of the horizon, moving at supersonic speeds on a desperate race for freedom.

29

Below them now, the high mountain valley belched fire and smoke like a volcano preparing to erupt.

The covert base was convulsed in spasms of destruction as munitions and fuel stores cooked off and sent contrails of fire and cascades of sparks geysering high into the black night sky.

Cox hoped that the vasaltnickis were now doing the prudent thing and hauling their asses out of the hot zone before local militia came into the area.

If they were caught, their lives would be worth precious little. With the Russian Republic in a state of utter chaos, their official sanction from Moscow Center meant little or nothing, and in fact might even count against them.

Regardless of how the Russians fared, Cox had his own priorities to deal with now. The vasaltnickis had helped get him and Gilroy airborne, but their chances of making it back to Svalbard Island alive were still highly questionable.

With the Blackbird now lightened by several hundred pounds due to the multimillion-dollar photoreconnaissance and ELINT equipment which he and Gilroy had jettisoned prior to takeoff, the SR would require less fuel and would additionally enjoy a higher margin for success.

But it was at best a slim margin, and one which,

under any other circumstances, Cox would not accept as workable even on a dare.

Navigating by GPS, Cox saw the horizon line fall away as he executed a ninety-degree turn and pointed the Blackbird's nose on a northwesterly course heading.

For the remainder of the trip, the SR-71 would be under Cox's hands-on control; there would be no more flying by wire.

The skies above Russia would be a danger zone and the SR could turn into a target of opportunity at any moment. Cox knew that the sooner he reached the plane's ninety-thousand-foot flight ceiling, the safer he and Gilroy would be from enemy interception.

Cox pushed the throttle forward and the Blackbird screamed higher and higher on full afterburner, spreading her night-black wings and sending a double-sonic boom rolling across the ancient Russian hills as the spyplane soared toward the upper reaches of space.

Flight commander Lev Borovich sat beside a console on which multiple-mode display screens showed a constantly shifting picture of the airspace above the northern Commonwealth of Independent States.

The MOSS electronic surveillance aircraft's pylon-mounted elliptical section rotodome slowly revolved above the fuselage of the Russian AWACS craft, its powerful liquid-cooled, over-the-horizon radars searching the skies.

Borovich had placed the ELINT crew of the TU-126 aircraft on full alert. The distress signal that had been received on a constantly monitored SAR channel a short while ago had brought startling news. Its implications were amazing.

There was no doubt that the distress call had originated from the secret base commanded by General

Fyodor Aleksiev which was located high in the fastness of the northern mountains.

No response had been received even after repeated attempts, and soon reports filtering in from ground-based forward observers indicated that a series of massive explosions had been set off in that exact location.

Ground forces were already moving in to reconnoiter the situation. Borovich was certain that these troops would discover the base to be laid in ruins.

If this were to prove to be the case, as it almost certainly would, then it would mean that the ambitious plot hatched by Aleksiev had been quashed. Such an outcome would also mean that Borovich's own safety would then be seriously compromised.

Borovich cursed himself for having been drawn into the web of conspiracy woven by Aleksiev. He had been a fool and soon might be held accountable for his folly.

The conspiracy was deeply embedded in the uppermost levels of the Russian military hierarchy and the Congress of Deputies alike, and it was possible that those on the fringes of the mutiny might escape retribution.

However, Borovich's past ties with Aleksiev—dating back to the campaign in Afghanistan and even before that—were a matter of public record. He would undoubtedly be one of the first to be questioned by the KGB, which would be looking for scapegoats to save its members' own necks.

Damn the general! thought Borovich. Damn him to—

"Commander, I want to inform you that radar contact has been established with an American spyplane."

Borovich immediately snapped out of his reverie at the message which crackled over the intercom grille located to his left. He picked up the console handset and punched in the lighted button, connecting himself to the R/O's station farther aft.

"Are you certain?" he asked the radar officer.

"There is no question about the sighting, sir," the R/O responded immediately. "The radar signature of the aircraft is identical to that of the SR-71 which was encountered earlier."

"Another spyplane?" Borovich mused aloud as he punched up the radar image on one of the screens in front of him. Amazingly enough, there it was, the signature clearly and distinctly that of the SR aircraft.

"I doubt it, sir," the R/O returned, looking into his track prioritization scope. "Its course is taking it north, away from our airspace."

What was going on? Borovich asked himself.

The American spyplane had been forced down by Captain Magadan days before. It had been brought by truck to the base, where Aleksiev's technicians were to have dismantled it for study of its electronic surveillance components and the sophisticated ALCM which the plane also carried.

But then the answer was already plain to Borovich. Incredible as it seemed, the American pilot had succeeded in flying the SR-71 out of the mountain stronghold!

He was undoubtedly at that moment making a desperate run toward the coast, hoping to escape from Russian airspace and back to an American base, probably located in Swedish or Norwegian waters, long-used takeoff sites for U.S. spyplane missions.

Of course, the American pilot had no chance of succeeding in this desperate bid for freedom, but then again, he had already brought off the impossible merely by having gotten the spyplane into the air. In any case, it was imperative that the American aircraft be destroyed immediately.

The safe return of the spyplane and its crew might well prove to be the catalyst which would galvanize an international inquiry into the roots of the mutiny engineered by Aleksiev.

Such a development would only bring further pressure on the KGB to hunt for scapegoats, and more of a chance for Borovich to be caught in the Komitet's dragnet.

"Scramble fighter-interceptors," Borovich shouted into the handset, which he now gripped with white-knuckled tension. "Make certain they understand their orders in no uncertain terms. They are to shoot the plane down on sight. Repeat: *they are to shoot it down!*"

Captain Magadan received the orders with a mixture of astonishment and pleasure in equal proportions.

There was nothing to conclusively indicate as yet that the target aircraft was one and the same SR-71 which he had brought to a forced landing only forty-eight hours before.

Yet he knew in his bones that it was indeed the same plane.

If this turned out to be so, then Magadan would now be granted the chance to do what he should have been permitted to do originally. The orders left no doubt whatsoever this time: the spyplane was to be shot down, blown out of the skies completely.

With the SU-27 Flanker already warmed up by the ground crew, Magadan climbed into the fighter's cockpit and dogged down its Plexiglas bubble.

He throttled the plane up to full power and soon the fighter aircraft was screaming into the skies, an eagle of the steppes on the hunt for its unarmed American prey.

30

The first of the threat icons flashed to life on the Blackbird's long-range radar display as the pulse doppler main beam got a good "skin paint" on a bogey.

On TWS mode, the screen quickly registered several more.

All data indicated to Cox that the bogeys on the tail of the Blackbird were high-speed Russian fighter-interceptors. These were now located at the outermost limits of radar range; however, they were quickly closing on the Blackbird's position and would soon be able to launch a standoff missile strike.

Cox immediately put the SR-71 into a forty-five-degree wingover, pulling g's as the plane canted earthward and nosed east, then west on an evasive pattern. Another glance at the long-range radar display showed that Cox's maneuvers had not fazed the fighters, which had performed aerobatics to match his own evasive tactics and were continuing to close on their target.

Hamstrung by the plane's critical shortage of fuel reserves, Cox could not afford to put the Blackbird through the more energy-intensive maneuvers he had in his bag of tricks.

He was also aware that this time around, the interceptor pilots would have scrambled into the air armed with orders to shoot down his plane. As soon as the Blackbird was in range of the Russian fighters' standoff weapons, terminally guided aerial submunitions would bring her down quickly.

This eventuality had been considered by Cox, and he had decided on the sole course of action if indeed it materialized.

The Russians' battle doctrine differed significantly from that of American pilots insofar as the chain of command was rigidly enforced. The shoot-down of a Japan Airlines flight over Sakhalin Island in 1983 had yielded a wealth of insight into this "top-down" policy of engagement.

Since pilots were not trained to exercise a high degree of autonomy in their prerogatives when dealing with the contingencies of a combat situation, the Russian chain of command was highly vulnerable to a strategy of decapitation.

If Cox could take out the command, control, communications and intelligence strongpoint to which the fighter pilots were linked, then he might be able to throw a spanner into the works.

That C^{3}I strongpoint was the TU-126 advance warning and surveillance systems aircraft, which Cox saw represented as a glowing threat icon on the periphery of the long-range radar display screen. If Cox were able to neutralize the Russian MOSS aircraft, then he might buy himself the precious time necessary to elude the fighters on the SR's tail.

But he would have to act quickly in order to carry off this proactive strategy of defense. Flying on afterburner, the jet interceptors were closing rapidly and the SR would soon be within range of their standoff weapons systems.

Punching in a series of commands on the keypad beside his main tactical systems screen, Cox initialized the Highwire air-launched cruise missile which was carried in the internal weapon bay of the SR-71.

He was now glad that he had decided not to deploy the ALCM during the final encounter with the Russian fighters resulting in the forced landing of the SR-71.

Without recourse to using the missile at this present time, it would be a virtual certainty that the Blackbird would be taken down by the pursuit interceptors.

When the tactical systems display flashed the message that the Highwire was fully initialized, Cox input the command parameters which would download the coordinates of the TU-126 AWACS craft into the microprocessor-based inertial navigation and guidance system of the ALCM.

The high-speed target data migration procedure was concluded within seconds, upon which Cox received a second message confirming that the guidance data had been successfully downloaded and requesting Cox to input secondary target parameters in the event that the first target was not acquirable. Cox declined and instead armed the Highwire ALCM and input a command line to execute an immediate launch sequence.

Two panels on the underchassis of the Blackbird slid apart and hydraulic actuators extended the ALCM a few inches beneath the fuselage of the SR.

At once, the missile's solid fuel propellant ignited with a characteristic spluttering flame and the cruise missile sped toward the nose of the SR-71, then abruptly made a three-hundred-sixty-degree course correction as its navigational system locked onto the target's memory-mapped coordinates and thrust-vectored the ALCM in the appropriate direction, spewing a dense contrail of billowing exhaust gases in its wake.

Cox now shifted his glance from the GPS display, which relayed the SR-71's elevation, speed and position, to the long-range radar data reflected on his nondedicated screens and then to the computer-linked video display terminal, which would bring him real-time phototelemetry of the ALCM's progress toward the MOSS aircraft.

As the Russian interceptors continued to close the gap between themselves and the Blackbird, the Highwire ALCM streaked across the sky toward the MOSS platform, which was directing the fighters toward their target.

While Cox maintained an uneasy vigil on his screens, the R/Os stationed inside the crew compartment of the TU-126 were also paying close attention to the unexpected development that had suddenly shaped the battle in a new and heretofore unforeseen manner.

"Sir." Commander Lev Borovich heard the voice of the chief R/O, which now came from the speaker grille. "The enemy aircraft has just launched a missile. This aircraft appears to be its target!"

Borovich punched in commands that would echo the radar data on the R/O's scope on the display console in front of him. In confirmation, the crew chief saw the missile's threat icon glowing on the constantly refreshed face of the VDT and ordered the MOSS pilot to take immediate evasive action.

"Sir, the missile is matching our course." The R/O's voice came back a few minutes later. "Evasive maneuvers are having no effect."

Sweat broke out on Borovich's upper lip. He intuitively realized what the enemy pilot was trying to achieve.

The American was going for a decapitation strike!

It was a brilliant strategy. The TU-126 was unarmed, and against a brilliant warhead it was completely vulnerable.

Borovich picked up the console phone and issued immediate orders for the fighter-interceptors pursuing the SR-71 to change course and shoot down the terminally guided cruise.

* * *

Cox's features drew back into a tight, mirthless grin when he saw the sudden course change reflected in his long-range radar, which showed the threat icons suddenly shift direction as they broke formation and went after the deadly robotic round.

As the fighter jets wheeled sharply to pursue their new target, Cox now pulled g's and executed fresh evasive maneuvers, momentarily free from the long-range electronic scrutiny of his determined pursuers.

In the cockpit of the lead Sukhoi interceptor, Captain Yuri Magadan closely watched the blip on his radar scope which identified the rapidly closing ALCM.

Neither he nor the other pilots flying formation with him dared to deploy their heat-seeking missiles for fear of hitting one another in the process, and the memory of the fratricide which the American's tactics had brought about earlier was still painfully fresh in Magadan's mind.

Instead they would now have to rely on the firepower of their 23 mm Vulcan cannons. However, against a small, highly mobile and rapidly vectoring target such as the just-launched American ALCM, Magadan did not set much store in the effectiveness of this tactic.

Now the Russian fighters made visual contact with the Highwire ALCM, speeding past them at three o'clock.

Steeply banking his plane as he peeled out of formation and diving toward the deadly little robot bomb, Magadan was the first pilot to attempt an interception of the brilliant round, and fired a salvo of automatic cannon fire at it.

Predictably, the interception maneuver proved to be unsuccessful, and Magadan's failure to blow the ALCM out of the air was repeated by each successive attempt on the part of the other planes in the pursuit formation.

Not only were their weapons inadequate to effect the destruction of the brilliant round, but the pilots had not been trained in this sort of maneuver, which was beyond the performance specifications of the aircraft they flew as well.

"Unable to effect destruction of the incoming missile," Magadan radioed the MOSS platform. "Regrettably, it proved impossible."

"Continue with interception," came Borovich's reply from the forward cabin of the Russian AWACS craft.

Having broken communication with the fighter wing, Borovich received a position update from the MOSS R/O which brought the dismaying news that the ALCM was closing fast and would soon be within range of a proximity-fuzed airburst. "Initialize ECM procedures immediately!" Borovich ordered.

The SIGINT officer immediately put the electronic countermeasures order by Borovich into effect, sending out noise and repeater jamming signals, which were designed to spoof the sensors of the incoming round and cause it to veer from its true target by creating the electronic equivalent of a room full of mirrors in a "gate-stealing" deception ploy.

However, the brilliant ALCM had inbuilt ECCM— electronic counter-countermeasure filters—engineered into its microprocessor-based guidance system, and its target lock was not perturbed by the false pulse doppler transmissions put out by the MOSS.

ECM procedures having failed to cause a missile break lock, Borovich next ordered the immediate deployment of flares and dipole chaff—tiny streamers of aluminized glass fiber one-half wavelength long, which act as microwave reflectors—the only other defensive measures against enemy missiles which the TU-126 carried on board.

Linked by coded telemetry with the quickly closing round, Cox now had real-time video contact with the

Russian command-and-control plane on his tactical display scope.

Caught in the glowing kill box of the target sighting reticle which flashed on his VDT, Cox clearly saw the flank of the Russian AWACS craft.

Constantly changing numerals on the display panel indicated that the command-guided ALCM had now penetrated the inner envelope of its lethal burst radius.

The Blackbird pilot's features had hardened into a taut mask of intense concentration as he punched the red button at the edge of the tactical keypad and detonated the ALCM's high-explosive warhead.

The VDT raster immediately bloomed and the image blanked as the Highwire warhead exploded in an airburst of extremely high lethality.

Borovich heard the thunderous boom and saw a blast of bright, blinding light as the warhead detonated a few feet from where he sat.

The rogue mission commander was among the first casualties as a shock front of intense heat and blast energy pulsed through the rupture in the aircraft's hull and melted his eyeballs in their sockets and baked the flesh from his bones before his burned skeleton was smashed to flinders against the bulkheads of the plane.

Within a matter of seconds, the fierce blast wave had raced through the MOSS, the miniature fire storm melting steel and fusing silicon microprocessors as it set the signals intelligence crew ablaze in a burnout zone of blistering heat which utterly disintegrated the TU-126 in midair.

Moments later, nothing remained of MOSS except the telltale traces of smoke as fuel-soaked engine wreckage and jagged chunks of burning hull debris sailed aimlessly through the sky and began a brief, final cascade to the mountainous terrain below.

31

Captain Magadan saw the strobing light of the multiple explosions illuminating the eastern sky.

It meant that the TU-126 MOSS had been destroyed!

By means of the same maneuver, the American pilot had bought himself vital lead time as the Russian interceptor jets turned from their attack vector to go chasing off after the missile round.

Magadan had to hand it to the American.

He was indeed the most formidable aviator he had ever encountered in his entire military career, his skill and daring exceeding the performance limitations of the aircraft he flew. To have survived as long as he had against such disproportionate odds was nothing short of incredible.

However, the American's luck had finally run out. With the TU-126 platform annihilated, the Sukhoi squadron would not have the benefit of its highly accurate telemetry to be sure.

Nevertheless, they were perfectly capable of finding, outmaneuvering and ultimately killing the Blackbird spyplane by means of their on-board battle management systems. It was only a matter of time before the inevitable happened.

Using his long-range radar, Magadan searched the skies for the fleeing SR-71. Before long, his air-combat acquisition search bore fruit.

There was the plane.

He now had it on his scope!

It had changed course several times and was now in another part of the sky and at a different altitude entirely from its last known sighting. But the Sukhois owned the skies, and as fast as the Blackbird might be, it was still no match for the superior speed and firepower of the Flankers.

"I've got the bandit on my scope," Magadan radioed to the other two pursuit aircraft, now two hundred nautical miles behind him. He communicated azimuth, elevation, range and velocity data to the other pilots in the squadron.

In the meantime, Magadan would go after the SR-71 alone.

The veteran pilot's eyes flicked to his fuel gauge, which showed the needle well forward of the halfway mark. He would have no difficulty in quickly closing the gap between the two aircraft and kicked in his afterburners, feeling the Sukhoi leap forward through space.

Approximately three hundred miles to the north, as it approached the limits of Russian territory, the Blackbird's track-while-scan threat display flashed the icon of the SU-27, the interceptor's course heading and pursuit speed indicating that the plane was closing on an intercept vector at multi-Mach speeds.

"Damn it! They've picked us up again," Cox said to Gilroy via the plane's on-board intercom.

"Well, look on the bright side, boss," she responded. "We're a couple of hundred pounds lighter now, aren't we?"

"Gilroy," Cox returned acidly, "I am one sorry sonofabitch. I've got the Russian air force closing in and Mary Sunshine sitting in my backseat."

"Love you too, boss," Gilroy replied.

Although it had been even money that the Russian fighters would attempt to close with them again in the wake of the destruction of the MOSS platform, Cox had hoped against his own better judgment that he would have been able to make it out of hostile airspace by then.

For the past several minutes, Cox had been sending out distress calls on the international emergency frequency, hoping to make contact with the Watchtower mission-support facility on Svalbard Island.

Cox knew full well that Holloway would have written the aircraft off to a Russian shoot-down after they had vanished from radar over two days before, but the possibility still existed that search-and-rescue aircraft and ships were continuing to be deployed.

So far his S.O.S. calls had received no response.

"Mayday, Mayday," Cox said into his commo unit, continuing to broadcast the distress signal. "This is Lookout. Come in, Crossroads. Repeat, this is Lookout. Come in, Crossroads."

Six hundred miles to the northeast, a radioman seated at his post on the CIA frigate stationed off the coast of Svalbard Island in Norwegian waters received the faint signal on the distress channel, which had been monitored constantly since the disappearance of the Watchtower flight crew nearly fifty hours before.

He immediately signaled for one of the comm room personnel to inform Holloway of the contact as he initialized fine-tuning, signal amplification and message recording procedures.

"Crossroads to Lookout," the radio officer said into the goosenecked mike at the communications station he manned, "what's your position?"

Cox and Gilroy both breathed a sigh of relief as Cox scanned his GPS display and relayed the coordinates beamed from Navstar one hundred fifty miles in low earth orbit to the radio officer on board the CIA frigate.

"We'll send Big Dipper over right away," the radio officer said. "You probably need a tall one right now."

"Negative," Cox replied. Big Dipper was the call sign for the Blackbird's dedicated KC-135Q tanker aircraft. But Cox knew that there was no chance of refueling the spyplane at this point. "Repeat. That's a negative. Big Dipper won't do us any good."

The needle of the SR's fuel gauge was already nosing down toward the red hash marks which indicated that the last of the plane's fuel reserves were depleted.

Starved for fuel, the spyplane's twin Pratt & Whitney turbo ramjet engines would flame out well before Cox could take on any more fuel from the airborne tanker ship. "We need Piranha instead. Repeat, we need Piranha urgently."

"I copy that, Lookout," the ground support installation's radioman acknowledged immediately.

Piranha referred to the squadron of F15E Strike Eagles that had been deployed to Svalbard Island in the event of precisely the kind of development which was taking place now.

The Strike Eagles were a measure of last resort because it was hoped that a dogfight with Russian aircraft would not materialize.

"Crossroads to Lookout," the CIA frigate radioman said into his console goosenecked mike. "Piranha are going into the water. Repeat, Piranha are going into the water. Good luck, Lookout. Crossroads out."

"Roger, Crossroads, and thanks," Cox said, terminating the communication.

He only hoped that the F15 squadron would not be too late to do them any good. A glance at the AN/APG-67 threat display indicated that the lead Sukhoi of the killer pack was rapidly closing the gap between itself and the SR-71.

Soon, Cox knew, the pursuit fighter would have them

within range of its ALAMO radar-guided missiles. He glanced at the GPS display and punched up the distance remaining before he and Gilroy would reach friendly airspace.

They would reach it soon, GPS assured him. But would it be soon enough?

In the cockpit of the Sukhoi, Captain Yuri Magadan checked the SU-27 fighter aircraft's long-range radar scope and received the indication that he was finally within the fighter's missile launch envelope.

Too far to use the plane's IR-seeking APHID missiles, but just close enough to deploy the longer-ranged, radar-homing ALAMO birds mounted in their conformal dispensers beneath the SU-27's wings.

Magadan had him!

Quickly selecting the AA-18 ALAMO missile by clicking its glowing electronic icon on the Sukhoi's tactical display, Magadan initiated launch and deployed the air-to-air terminally guided warhead with his radar set on single target track.

Moments later, he received confirmation that the precision-guided airborne munition was locked onto the radar backscatter reflected from the Sukhoi's phase comparison monopulse radar's skin paint on the Blackbird's fuselage and was homing in on the target aircraft.

A sudden burst of energy in the infrared caused the Blackbird's flash detector to pop a missile icon onto the radar scope now scanning in long-range mode.

The launch signature indicated that the lead Sukhoi, far closer than the other two jet fighters originally scrambled by MOSS, had fired a warhead at the SR-71.

From a glance at the target recognition scope, Cox realized that it must be a radar-seeking missile round.

The pilot was too far away at this point to have deployed an IR-chasing missile.

Cox threw the Blackbird into a three-g turn, then leveled off and turned again in a tightly executed maneuver intended to defeat the missile's radar lock. In the end, though, the ploy proved to be unsuccessful.

The round was still vectoring toward the SR, zigzagging to exactly match the course changes of its side-breaking target, the incoming warhead's signature growing progressively larger as the rocket neared its target.

There was no way to outrun the incoming missile; Cox knew this beyond a doubt. The warhead would easily overtake the SR and detonate for a proximity-fuzed airburst when the spyplane was within destructive range of its lethal blast radius.

The Blackbird was equipped with a "black box," however—an AN/ALQ-131 radar-jamming module—and Cox initialized the ECM system. But the continuing lock of the tracking Russian missile demonstrated that the ICM was equipped with effective electronic countermeasures and would not be defeated by AN/ALQ's noise and repeater jamming defensive strategies.

Only a single option remained to defeat such a radar-seeking threat, and that was to jink the agile black aircraft into the tracking radar's blind sector in order to break the target lock which the incoming round had on the SR.

Cox had only seconds in which to act and he knew he would get but a single shot at carrying out the desperate maneuver. Again he pulled g's, sideslipping the spyplane sharply to port before leveling out again moments before the round would reach its target.

Critical seconds ticked by, with Cox's radar scope still showing the missile closing. Nearer and nearer it came, until it was almost in range of airburst detonation.

"Sorry, kid," Cox began, knowing they were both about to die. "I—"

The threat icon on his AN/APG-67 screen suddenly vanished!

Cox had succeeded in breaking the missile's target lock, using aerial maneuvers to accomplish what the SR's "black box" could not.

Moments later, Cox saw the exhaust plume of the deflected missile veer off on a perpendicular track at three o'clock, followed by a sudden bright flash as the warhead exploded a millisecond later.

"You did it, boss!" Gilroy's voice shouted in his ear. "I wouldn't have believed it if I hadn't seen it for myself!"

"Save the congratulations for later, kid," Cox mirthlessly replied to his jubilant backseater. "We're still in serious trouble. That Sukhoi riding our tail's got more ordnance to throw at us, and in case you've forgotten, there are two other planes on our tail too."

Cox again checked the GPS display and saw that the SR-71 had closed the gap between them and their destination by several score miles since the Sukhoi had fired its homing round.

But the fuel gauge needle had already dropped into the red zone, indicating that the Blackbird was now completely out of fuel.

Moments later, Cox felt the entire craft kick like a bronc as the first of the SR's engines flamed out, echoed by the electronic warning tones which immediately began to sound in the cockpit.

The Blackbird's second engine flamed out a few moments later.

The SR-71 was now gliding through the skies without any means of propulsion, its engines cold, its stick dead and gravity pulling it toward the earth faster and faster with each moment that went by.

32

Svalbard Island

Minutes after Cox's distress signal had been received, the squadron of F15E Strike Eagles was airborne, the agile multirole combat aircraft screaming up into the cold blue sky on a flight vector which would take them into Russian airspace.

The pilots of the Strike Eagles had been briefed prior to takeoff on the necessity for speed and deadliness. An aerial dogfight between U.S. and Russian jets was a nightmare contingency that had plagued the planners of Watchtower.

Nevertheless, it was a contingency they had been forced to consider and one which they believed could be dealt with, the consensus among the mission planners being that the Kremlin would opt to play down the incident, if it arose, in the interests of overall deconfliction.

In the present state of the Russian national crisis, the need for bank loan guarantees had replaced political rhetoric, and the need to provide butter to the Russian masses would silence the guns of its saber-rattling military.

At the same time, surface craft were scanning the skies in case the Blackbird would be forced to ditch over water. In this event, Navy SEAL teams were standing ready and would be immediately deployed to rescue any survivors and retrieve whatever flight data was available.

Kicking in their afterburners, the F15s knifed through the skies at multi-Mach speeds, vectoring in on the targets which their long-range radars had already gotten solid locks on. The pilots of the Strike Eagles had been handpicked for both their warrior spirit and their combat experience.

All had logged multiple mission time over the skies of Iraq, and each of the three pilots was among the few American fliers who had gotten solid experience in air combat against Russian fighter planes by shooting them down over the hardware-jammed and electronically cluttered Iraqi airspace during the hundred-hour war.

The pilots were eager to face the challenge of a dogfight with Russian aircraft that were the F15's direct equivalent, manned by their own opposite numbers from the Russian Voiska Protivozdushnoi Oborny (VPVO), or Air Defense Forces.

The fliers had felt lingering doubts in their own minds as to whether or not the multiple mission kills they had racked up over Iraq had been a result of the superiority of their hardware and combat savvy over the Russian planes or the innate inferiority of the Iraqi pilots.

This time they knew there would be no question about the quality of their adversaries: the pilots would be the cream of the former Sov air force and the Sukhois they flew were among the best fighter hardware in the weapons inventory of the Russian Republic.

As the American planes penetrated Commonwealth airspace, Magadan's long-range radar picked up the bandits' signatures. By this time the other two friendly planes had caught up with his own aircraft and they were now flying in tight formation.

"Look sharp," Magadan told the fighter squadron. "These are American strike aircraft we're up against. I don't have to tell you that they are the best in the skies."

Magadan had held off on reacquiring and launching further rocket attacks on the Blackbird, having noted that the plane's speed had shown a sudden and drastic decrease, which to him could only indicate that the SR-71 had suffered engine flameout and was now coasting along in a state of nonpowered glide.

If this was the case—which it almost certainly was— then the squadron of Russian aircraft would not need rockets in order to shoot down the black stealth ship.

They were quickly closing with the SR-71 and would be able to down the American spyplane using standard 23 mm cannon fire at close range, each of them taking turns in sending glowing tracers slamming into the fuselage of the CIA plane and watching it break up as it went down.

Now, in fact, Magadan was able to visually discern the tiny black speck against the blue of the sky which he knew must be the Blackbird.

With his plane traveling at three times the speed of sound, Magadan rapidly closed with the SR-71 and in a heartbeat could clearly distinguish the unique silhouette of the Blackbird's blended-chine tail section with its slightly downward-canted engine nacelles.

Magadan noted immediately that the twin ramjet nacelles' tail cones appeared completely inactive.

It was just as he had surmised: the American spyplane's engines had stopped dead.

Her pilot had used up the final reserves of fuel and was now gliding through space, a feat which the construction of the spyplane and the lightness of its fuselage in the absence of a full fuel load made possible.

Magadan had heard that such planes were capable of

gliding for hundreds of miles with cold engines on completely empty tanks. But this particular Blackbird would not duplicate that remarkable feat.

Within minutes, it would be spiraling earthward in flames.

Savoring the nearness of the assured kill, Magadan radioed to his wingmen to hold their fire for a few minutes. He wanted to have some fun with the Blackbird first.

He wanted to savor the thrill of the kill.

"But, Captain," one of the squadron members radioed back, "the American fighters, they are closing on us fast. Why don't we—"

"Damn the Americans!" Magadan shouted. "I said hold your fire until I tell you to shoot!"

Having issued his orders, Magadan increased thrust and shot ahead, matching speed with the slowly flying SR-71 until the cockpit of his Flanker was almost directly abeam of the spyplane's.

The Russian pilot could now discern the American pilot seated at the SR's controls, his face dimly visible through the visor bubble of his protective pressurized helmet.

Magadan raised his gloved hands in a mocking salute to the American, then peeled off and nosed the Sukhoi downward in a steep ballistic dive.

Buffeted fiercely by the jetwash of the Sukhoi as it vanished from view, Cox fought to keep the Blackbird stable as she glided without engines through the turbulent air. Turning his head, he could make out the nose assemblies of the two other fighter craft trailing the Blackbird to port and starboard.

"What are they doing?" asked Gilroy over the aircraft's intercom, her voice tense. "Why don't they just shoot and get it over with?"

"They're having some fun with us first," Cox rasped

back at her. "The dirt bags are going to toy with us before they shoot us down. They probably figure they can blast us out of the skies and turn tail before the F15s get close enough to engage. Once we're out of the picture, it won't be too likely that our guys will follow the Russians into the Russian heartland."

As if in confirmation of his judgment call, Cox heard a sudden peal of mechanical thunder, and the Blackbird was rocked savagely by the fierce turbulence of air displaced by the Sukhoi careening past the SR-71 at supersonic speed.

Cursing the Russian pilot, Cox fought the stick to keep the Blackbird from barrel-rolling out of control as the lightweight aircraft was severely pummeled by the shock wave of sudden overpressure like a small vessel caught in a raging ocean swell.

Now, following Magadan's lead, the other two Russian warplanes each peeled out of formation, buffeting the Blackbird with their jetwash as they put their planes into steep ballistic dives before standing the Sukhois on their tails and rocketing skyward again on full afterburner to slam vortices of compressed air and sonic vibration against the fuselage of the spyplane which hit with the force of successive hammerblows.

This severe punishment went on for several minutes until Magadan grew weary of the deadly game. It was now time to finish off the Blackbird. The American F15s were closing fast and would soon be reaching their position.

As long as they remained in close proximity with the SR-71, there would be virtually no danger of the Americans deploying their rockets because of the risk in blowing up the Blackbird in the process.

But once the Sukhois were within range of their standoff weapons systems, such as Sparrow and Sidewinder, the F15s would close in for a dogfight without a doubt.

Magadan was at the top of his climb now, having careened dangerously close to the SR-71 on his last flyby.

Now he nosed the SU-27 into a steeply angled dive and closed his finger over the fire button of his wing strake-mounted 23 mm cannon.

When his HUD caught the SR in the center of his target acquisition reticle, Magadan depressed the fire button on his joystick, aiming for the cockpit canopy as the heavy-caliber tracer rounds streaked through space.

Magadan uttered a Russian oath as he suddenly saw the Blackbird jink left and right, however, and saw the tracers narrowly miss the cockpit to smash instead into the center portion of the SR's fuselage, a point in the aircraft's chined hull which, now devoid of fuel and weaponry, housed no critical components.

The American had pulled the last trick out of his bag, the Russian promised himself.

Magadan's next salvo of 23 mm fire would vector solidly into the SR's cockpit and take off the pilot's head.

He leveled out the Flanker and once again got the Blackbird's nose assembly centered in his target scope.

Magadan's finger hovered over the joystick-mounted fire button. In another moment he would send the black stealth plane into a terminal spiral, terminating in a nonsurvivable crash.

The moment never arrived.

Suddenly Magadan's own aircraft had come under fire as the F15 Strike Eagles streaked across the Russian skies and leveled bursts of their own Vulcan cannons at his Sukhoi.

Magadan saw the glowing white tracer rounds whisk past his cockpit and reflexively whipped the Sukhoi sharply to starboard on a high-g turn to avoid a direct hit by the now heavily incoming Vulcan fire.

As he performed this sudden pullout maneuver, he saw the sleek black nose assembly of the Blackbird fall away to one side of his forward horizon and the escaping SR wiggle her wings mockingly.

Anger boiled inside Magadan's blood because he had bungled the chance to down the spy craft through his own consuming eagerness for revenge, and he knew that when it was all over, he would face severe repercussions for these actions.

But just now his priorities had changed entirely.

Survival against the agile and lethal Strike Eagles was uppermost in his mind.

After making a tight turn, Magadan applied thrust and sent the Sukhoi streaking skyward, attempting to simultaneously gain altitude on the attacking American aircraft and turn his own plane into the sun to blind the attack force pilots.

At the same time, the other two Sukhois in his squadron had been engaged by the American planes, and all combatants realized that they were each in for the fight of their lives.

All of a sudden there was a thunderous explosion below Magadan, a fireball of blinding luminescence which filled the entire sky.

Craning his neck, Magadan looked down over the side of his cockpit bubble to see that one of the Sukhois in his formation had just been struck broadside by a rocket and had exploded into a mass of flames.

There was no sign of the pilot's parachute opening.

He had not had time to bail out.

As one of the F15s went after the other surviving SU-27, the other two American warplanes double-teamed him. Magadan saw both fighter craft framed in the target acquisition reticle of his head-up display and initiated two APHID IR-seeking missiles.

When the first plane was locked in the kill box of his head-up display, he deployed the missiles. The APHIDs streaked from their underwing-mounted weapon dispensers and vectored in on the exhaust nozzle of the targeted American jet.

Both F15Es peeled off to opposite sides of the sky as the target aircraft took evasive action in an attempt to shake off the tail-pipe-chasing APHIDs.

There was no hope for the targeted aircraft, however. The APHIDs were locked onto its IR signature as they closed in for the kill.

In seconds they reached their target and their proximity-fuzed warheads detonated. As the F15E went up in a brief but blinding fireball, Magadan felt gratified. The kill had evened the score for the downing of one of his own men in the dogfight.

However, the Blackbird was now well beyond his grasp.

The American pilot had succeeded in evading him for the last time, Magadan knew. With the F15Es having entered the picture, there now remained no hope of bringing it down, and with the SR's escape made good, the reason for continuing the dogfight no longer existed.

Indeed, Magadan's priority now lay in saving his own neck from the dangerous political repercussions of his having taken part in the general's mutiny putsch, and that end would only be thwarted by continuing the aerial combat.

"Return to base immediately! Engage enemy aircraft only if they pursue," he ordered the surviving Sukhois as he firewalled the Flanker's afterburner and disengaged, certain that the Americans would not dare to strike deeper into Russian territory unless further provoked.

Magadan was proven right as the pilots at the controls of the F15Es watched the two surviving Flankers streak away and then turn in the sky and vanish in the direction from which the SR-71 had flown.

Despite his own anger, Magadan suddenly recalled the words to an American song he had once heard, and he smiled dourly at the appropriateness of its central lyrics.

"Bye-bye, blackbird," the words had gone.

33

Cox saw the two target recognition icons on his AN/APG-67 scope close quickly. For a moment he wondered if they were Sukhois giving chase, but then he saw the familiar profiles of the two F15E Strike Eagles materializing to port and starboard of the Blackbird's cockpit.

"The Russians have turned back," the lead pilot radioed to Cox. "We each lost a plane. I guess the tangos figured that it evened the score."

"Roger," Cox said to the pilot. "Good going. You guys pulled our chestnuts out of the fire."

"That's what we get paid for, guy," the squadron leader returned in no-sweat tones.

All three aircraft had now cleared the Russian landmass and were soaring flat out over the open ocean below.

The F15E pilots saw that the Blackbird's angle of descent, which had been slow but stable up until now, was beginning to deteriorate sharply as the craft lost the added lift provided by thermal air currents rising off the land surface.

"Your glide slope is beginning to decay badly," the fighter squadron leader radioed Cox. "Advise you ditch in the ocean as soon as possible. We'll fly a holding pattern and radio coordinates to the SEAL search team currently standing down."

"Negit on that," Cox radioed back to the fighter jockey. "I'm taking this baby in for a landing on Svalbard. I think I can keep her stable all the way down the slot."

"You'll never make it," the fighter pilot argued, a new edge in his voice. "You're losing altitude too quickly. Ditch in the drink. Repeat, ditch in the drink. Over."

"Negative," Cox said again. "We're going in all the way or no way. And that's what *I'm* paid for, baby-cakes. Right, Mary Sunshine?"

"Whatever you say, boss," Gilroy replied.

Cox didn't have the time or the inclination to explain to the fighter jockey his reasons for risking his and Gilroy's lives on a desperate bid to land the plane on the forward observation base's runway. It would have taken too long to do, and besides, he could never fully and accurately communicate the reasons for his actions anyway.

In truth, Cox could not put his finger on many of them himself, except that to have come this far and not have completed the circle would be to leave a question hanging in his mind for the rest of his life: could he have done it? However others might judge him, Cox was certain that his Balinese friends would both understand and approve of his decision.

Suddenly there was a new voice coming over the SR's radio.

"Lookout, this is Crossroads," the voice of the Watchtower ground commander said. "I'm ordering you to ditch in the sea. Do you copy that, Lookout? Ditch the bird in the drink. That's an order."

"*Shove* your order, Holloway," Cox returned. "I'm taking the SR in for a landing. You sent us in shoulder-ing all the risks and with no damn support, and you're going to get us back the same way. If I were you," he continued, "I'd be lining up an emergency crew right about now."

Cox added, "The emergency crew's for you, by the way, because I'm gonna break your fucking jaw as soon as I land this bird."

There was a long beat of silence during which Cox heard the crackling static of dead air coming over the radio transceiver. Then Holloway's voice returned on-line once again.

"All right, Lookout, you dumb, stubborn sonofabitch, have it your way," Holloway said angrily. "The ground crew's already waiting. Over to you, Lookout."

"Wilco on that," Cox replied. "And one more thing. Have a bottle waiting for me when I see you. And let a smile be your umbrella. Lookout over and out."

Cox next spoke to Gilroy over the spyplane's intercom. "Hang on, kid," he told her. "It's gonna get hairy."

"Anything you say, boss," Gilroy's voice responded. "You've got the ball. At this point I'm just along for the ride."

By this point the Blackbird was losing altitude faster and faster as its glide slope continued to rapidly decay. Cox's altimeter showed that in the past few seconds he'd already dropped several thousand feet.

Only a rough ten thousand feet separated the underbelly of the SR-71 from the choppy surface of the ocean, and at the rate that its descent profile was deteriorating, he figured that he would hit the surface in only about ten minutes. At the speeds the SR was traveling, this would result in approximately the same outcome as hitting a brick wall.

But Cox could now also see the coastline of Svalbard Island through the inch-thick windscreen of the Blackbird, and he knew that he would be able to bring the SR in for a landing in under five minutes.

That would be cutting it close by the finest possible margin, but Cox also was confident that he could beat the odds against survival: hell, it was practically getting to be a hobby by now, he thought with a smile.

Cox extended his landing gear as the Blackbird angled down ever more sharply and rapidly as it neared the ocean.

Now, minutes after his colloquy with the ground crew chief, the Blackbird scudded over the slowly revolving radar masts of the CIA frigate anchored off the island's shoreline, and Cox banked the Blackbird around to bring it directly into line with the covert runway.

Normally still at high Mach numbers on landing, the spyplane would announce its approach with its signature double sonic boom. But the SR's terminal velocity had slowed significantly and the Blackbird was coming down for its landing at uncharacteristic subsonic speeds.

Below, emergency vehicles were already waiting on the sidelines, their circus lights flashing, ready to race in after the crash landing which each member of the rescue teams expected.

Flying the needle, Cox brought his altimeter centerline level with the artificial horizon of the spyplane's instruments and straightened out the Blackbird's double delta wings as the SR's landing gear completed their extension and locked fully into touchdown position.

He would deploy the Blackbird's drag chute at the last possible moment, hoping that it would slow the aircraft sufficiently for it to stop before he ran out of runway and went crashing into one of the prefabricated buildings which had been set up to house the installation's ground support personnel and equipment.

The Blackbird lurched back and forth as it was buffeted by the cushion of turbulent air thrown up by its passage at high speed over the runway. Like a spear in flight, the spyplane hurtled above the deck on a low-angle trajectory, and Cox raised his outboard wing elevons to increase drag and further reduce speed.

Much slower now with the increased wing resistance of the upward-canted control surfaces of its wings, the SR still streaked forward at hundreds of miles per hour. Then the landing gear bit into the tarmac with a series of loud screeches, and Cox and Gilroy bounced hard in their seats.

"Don't piss your pants, kid. I'm popping the drag chute," Cox said and pulled the stirrup control which would open the special doors of a compartment on the upper part of the fuselage empennage holding the chute in place and allow it to extend from the aircraft's tail section and fully deploy behind the speeding SR.

As soon as he did this, there was an audible *crack* as the deployed chute blossomed suddenly at the end of its tether. This full deployment of the drag chute was followed by a stomach-turning jolt as the chute scooped up enormous quantities of air and slowed the plane's forward momentum by hundreds of feet per second in a beat of the human pulse.

Now the Blackbird had all three landing gear on the blacktop, but Cox saw that the SR was running out of runway just the same. Only a short distance ahead of the Blackbird's nose assembly, the side of the big Quonset hut which served as the base command-and-control center was coming up fast.

The structure was looming up directly in the plane's forward line of approach, growing bigger and bigger with each passing second, and Cox knew that the SR would not be able to stop before its nose assembly went crashing through the building's walls, folding like an accordion bellows in the process and crushing both members of its flight crew to pulp.

"We're not going to make it, boss," Gilroy shouted. "Nice try, but I'm afraid you blew it."

"Yes, we will, kid." Cox raised the SR's left wing flap to send the Blackbird suddenly skewing hard to starboard only a short distance before the runway gave out entirely. "We are *definitely* going to make it!"

The effect of this sudden maneuver was to counteract the aircraft's forward momentum and send the Blackbird fishtailing hard around, its tail section whipping into the position which its nose had occupied only a moment before.

With virtually any other military aircraft short of a light reconnaissance plane, this gambit would have proved suicidal, but Cox was pinning his hopes on two factors unique to the aircraft he was flying.

The first was the fact that the Blackbird, minus its load of JP-7 fuel, was extremely light in weight for its size. The second factor was a far less tangible one: he had hoped that the SR's forward speed had slowed the plane to the point where the desperate maneuver would not terminate in a fatal flip-over.

Time froze in a heart-stopping moment as the Blackbird's forward landing gear slipped from the blacktop surface of the runway tarmac and the plane lurched precariously downward, to come to a halt with its nose assembly jammed into the soft earth on the graded flanks of the runway and its deployed drag chute billowing at the end of its tether in the brisk sea wind like some giant red jellyfish.

But the SR-71 had stopped moving.

It had come to a complete halt!

Cox had landed the plane and he and his backseater were both miraculously alive.

Moments later, Cox and Gilroy were scrambling

from the SR's crew compartments as the emergency unit helped pilot and RSO down to the deck.

"I'm all right," Cox told the medics, waving them away as he took off his flight helmet and turned to look at the SR while other rescue personnel clustered around Gilroy.

His eyes followed the three parallel lines of rubber, which the spyplane's landing gear had laid down on the clandestine runway, to where the markings made a sudden loop, then came to an abrupt halt at the edge of the airstrip, where the Blackbird's sharply pointed tail section now angled up in the air.

Again the SR christened *Ichi Ban* had proved itself to be the most remarkable aircraft ever flown, Cox thought to himself. They might build them faster, but they would never build them any better.

She was a one-in-a-million airplane.

Cox turned back to the runway in time to see a Humvee drive up amid a cloud of dust. Holloway got out of its cab and began walking toward Cox, whose face now cracked a broad grin. There was a bottle of whiskey clutched by the neck in Holloway's hand.

EPILOGUE

Rome

Boris Tallin dragged on the Gauloise Blue as he leaned across the balustrade of smooth white stone.

Burnished to a slick patina by centuries of being rubbed by the sleeves of the sightseers and strollers who had rested their arms there, the balustrade cordoned off the section of the Borghese Gardens just above the Spanish Steps, a position from which he could look down upon the rooftops of the city below.

Since his arrival in Rome a month before, Tallin had gotten into the habit of returning to this particular spot quite often.

When the sun was just right, the great cantilevered dome of St. Peter's Basilica was lit by an almost unearthly luminescence and the many bridges crossing the Tiber all seemed to be made out of burnished gold.

The view of the Eternal City had a calmative effect on his mind, representing many things to him. Above all else was freedom, something which Tallin had not been able to taste for a long time.

Now, as he leaned on the balustrade and ran his eye across the rooftops of downtown Rome, which he often did on such occasions, Tallin's mind drifted back to the final mission he had undertaken in his homeland.

His vasaltnicki team had encountered the expected

fierce resistance as militia forces converged on the destroyed mountain stronghold, and many of his best men had not made it back.

Saddest of all, the roster of the dead had included Mikhail and Gennady, two of the best soldiers and the bravest comrades whom it had ever been Tallin's privilege to know and fight alongside.

There had been a period of turmoil during which it appeared that anything might happen, but in the end, the Center was able to reassert its power and the republics remained united, albeit uneasily.

With the conspirators who had supported the Aleksiev mutiny hounded by the Komitet, it had become a mad contest to see which of them could turn the others in faster.

The knowledge that some of the selfsame Mossoviet and GRU big shots who had thrown him into prison to rot were now doing time in Lefortovo was one of the more pleasant outcomes of the entire business.

Those at the top of the chain of command had no chance, not with the Americans and Europeans in direct complicity with those who would profit by keeping drawn the veil of secrecy which had fallen over the whole stinking enterprise.

As Tallin had predicted all along, it was in the interests of nobody at all to turn Aleksiev's abortive coup d'état into a global circus or national inquisition.

As for himself and his vasaltnickis, Tallin had made certain that they would all be well compensated for their service to Mother Russia and to the rest of the world.

The cache of gold bars which had been plundered from the coffers of Kabul by the late and unlamented General Fyodor Ivan'ch Aleksiev almost fifteen years before was now sitting securely in a bank vault beneath the streets of Zurich, Switzerland.

The millions of dollars in bullion would provide lifetime annuities for Tallin and the men who had served with him on the final mission, both those living and those who had been killed in action in Afghanistan and the Russian heartland.

For the latter, their families would suffer no privations. Their sacrifices would not have been completely in vain.

Pavlovich had given his tacit approval to Tallin's use of the gold, and its loss to the coffers of the Russian treasury was a small price for the Kremlin to pay to ensure the continued secrecy of·Tallin and his surviving men.

As far as the Americans were concerned, Tallin had heard that they were reexamining their near-total reliance on orbiting spy satellites to provide them with the intelligence which was vital to maintaining the fragile East-West peace alliance and preserving the new balance of power which had developed in the wake of glasnost, perestroika and the August coup.

Regarding the SR-71, the spyplane was to be revamped and once again to become part of the U.S. intelligence-gathering mission.

The sun was beginning to set now, and Tallin's thoughts turned back to the few fleeting minutes he had spent with the American pilot who had undertaken the daring mission of flying the SR-71 Blackbird into Commonwealth airspace.

He had learned later of how the American had eluded the Russian interceptor aircraft and survived an air-to-air missile attack to make a successful dead-stick landing at the secret CIA forward observation base.

There, thought Tallin, was a man he could respect, a man with whom he felt a kinship which transcended distance, language and national boundaries.

They would meet, the two of them, Tallin had decided, and on that day they would drink a toast of good *pertsovka* vodka to the folly of their leaders and to the bravery of men who dared the impossible. They would both surely have great stories to tell!

As the sun set behind the ancient skyline of Rome, Tallin flicked the butt of his cigarette into the cooling, gold-tinged air and turned away from the balustrade. There was an interesting cafe on the Piazza Navona where he had dined the night before, and his evening's stroll had given him a hearty appetite.

Life was good when men were free, thought Tallin as he turned back toward the Spanish Steps, and freedom was a cause worth defending at any price. Without it, life was nothing.